The Other Door

The Other Door

Karen Heuler

an imprint of

MANOR

Rockville, Maryland

Some of the stories in this collection first appeared in the following publications: "The Hole Story," in Beloit Fiction Journal; "Like a Piston, Like a Flame," in Crosscurrents; "The Revolt of Everyday Things," in The Massachusetts Review; "Overpowering Joy," in Ms.; "Simple Accommodations," in New Virginia Review; and "Ghost Nets," in TriQuarterly, a publication of Northwestern University.

This is a work of fiction.

ISBN: 978-1-64973-159-3

www.PhoenixPick.com

Phoenix Pick Edition, October 2025.

Published by Phoenix Pick
an imprint of Arc Manor
P. O. Box 10339
Rockville, MD 20849-0339
www.ArcManor.com

Contents

Like A Piston Like A Flame

Vera lost her legs on the way to work when a cornice fell from a thirty-second-floor window. It missed Vera but hit the back of a truck heading west on Fifty-sixth Street, causing momentary confusion and an impulsive swerve onto the sidewalk, where Vera was hurrying, toes out, on her way to a performance.

The doctor told her she would never dance again. The physical therapist told her that with artificial legs she could continue to lead a normal life. "My normal life is dancing," Vera replied.

Vera had ghost pains in the legs she no longer had. She also had ghost arabesques, ghost plies, ghost muscle cramps. At times she wasn't sure when she was dreaming and when she wasn't. But at heart, Vera was a realist. When she was fitted with wooden legs—the latest model, with flexible joints and movable toes—she spent two days just sitting on her bed and looking at them.

The nurses were nonplussed because they depended on Vera to be a model patient. She could be used as an example for the whiners on the ward, for the bell-pushing, angry-eyed, self-pitying others. Vera set up a standard of rational behavior for tragedy; she did not ask "Why this? Why me?"

Could it be that Vera was, after all, just as human as the others? Would she end up moaning in the darkness? Was that why she froze thoughtfully as soon as her new legs appeared? Was denial invading her bed?

1

But Harry, Vera's husband, knew the reason. "She is deciding what to do with them," he said, and he nodded his head in approval.

Harry was a carny man; he was a fire-eater. The poster that introduced him claimed he was the best in the world, but that poster made no mention of the various tricks Harry did in private that he kept to himself. Vera knew, of course.

Their mutual respect for privacy, individuality, and the high creative arts stood them well and came in handy. Working in the circus, Harry was often out of town. Working in the ballet, so was Vera. They had a large loft in midtown Manhattan where they would celebrate their reunions by performing for each other—Vera inciting the air with her astonishing leaps; Harry spitting out fire, swallowing it; the two of them improvising a spirited duet.

So when Vera sat on the edge of the hospital bed just staring at her wooden legs, she was estimating their range and talent—she was improvising again. They were her legs now; they would have to develop a mutual strategy. She was building a mental image of a dancer with legs such as these. She was letting the legs suggest what such a dancer might be.

Harry was working in New Jersey so he was able to spend most mornings with Vera, and he sat with her, nodding and building imagery of his own. He was also teaching himself to breathe differently, with less gusto, afraid lest a stray tongue of flame should lick out from his mouth and catch Vera's leg. Vera noticed it and smiled.

On the second day Vera rose and stepped gingerly on the hospital floor. She had no sense yet of where the new legs ended, and each step tested her judgment of distance and force. All the old instincts were useless, but what would the new ones bring? The wooden limbs tapped and scraped across the linoleum floor.

"Bring my ballet slippers," she told Harry.

They were now the wrong size for the wooden feet.

"I'll get you another pair," Harry said quickly, offended by this sign of inappropriateness. Surely the doctors should have found out what size her feet had been; what other errors would eventually be detected?

Vera covered his hand with hers. She beamed at him. "With bigger feet I may have better balance."

"Your balance was always perfect."

"And your tongue is always quick and light."

A little puff of pleasure drifted up from Harry's mouth.

Vera left the hospital with her wooden legs on her lap. Harry lifted her out of the wheelchair and found her body unfamiliar; it no longer draped the usual way.

Vera wasted no time. Back in the loft she pulled herself along the barre; she tried to plie in all the positions. She spent hours at it, falling and then pulling herself up. Harry huffed in the corner or in another room, trying not to notice. He accidentally singed his mustache, something he hadn't done in years. He spat out little whips of flame in misery and had to be warned to put them out.

"Especially with these wooden legs," Vera reminded him. "Especially now."

Harry flushed. "I'm careful," he claimed, a sizzle just barely making it from his lips.

"You're upset," Vera pointed out. "You lose control when you get emotional."

"I know that very well."

"You mustn't be upset. I'm not. I know I'll work it all out."

But Harry continued to be upset, quietly, wistfully upset. Circumstances contributed to it.

The first real visitors they had when Vera was well enough was a family from the carny who brought their four-year-old son, William.

William spent most of dinner under the table with his little hammer, tapping on Vera's feet. Everyone was horrified, but William crept back again and again. Vera was usually the last to notice; she only became alert to the tapping sounds when the stricken expressions on the faces around her left no alternative.

"It doesn't hurt, you know," she told them, but her guests left early, and Harry set a napkin on fire in distress.

Vera, flushed with annoyance, went back to the barre. She learned to plie; she learned to stand en pointe. Her extension was improved.

But no jêté.

"It's the calves," she said thoughtfully to Harry. "The muscles are no longer there. And I can't seem to relearn the other muscles quickly enough."

"It will come," Harry assured her, kneeling beside her.

"Harry, your breath!" she cried. A little trio of flames was hovering over her. Harry quickly swallowed them.

"Sorry."

"I have to find some way of doing it," she continued. "Springs or something."

"I'll talk to the clowns tomorrow," Harry said.

R. J., the lead clown, opened all the drawers in his chest and trunks. He pulled out large springs, small springs, springs with and without valves. He took out various hydraulic pumps, gaudily or neutrally colored. He nodded and smacked his lips all the while, murmuring things such as: "The expanding car; the bouncing fruit; the water that fell up." Yet when Harry protested that he didn't want to take away anything important, R. J. laughed. "They like the pratfalls best; they like the buckets of water that are really confetti. Anything else they feel belongs to the magicians. They want a rubber nose and a belief in superiority." He paused, suddenly annoyed. "And the magicians shall never get these."

So Harry left with springs and valves and hinges and wires. He gave them to Vera and kept himself from offering to help. He was an extremely delicate man: How do you help another person assemble her legs? Vera of course understood this delicacy, and furthermore approved of it.

Harry went back to the carny; Vera was well and working and would resent his solicitous presence. Besides, he had to work out his agitation-which was leaving far too many spurts of fire drifting around the apartment.

He worked on adding more intricate touches to his act. Of course the audience high in the tent could only appreciate the burning swords and pokers he swallowed and then blew out, but those in the front rows were treated to minor pyrotechnical wonders: to little balls of flames that were directed around the sword and to and from Harry's mouth; to fiery animals that ran along the edge of the poker and then disappeared. And then the juggler complained, and the animal trainer, that the crowds were only half as enthusiastic, and Harry was told to stop.

The day after Vera tried her first jêté., Harry expelled so much fire that he was enveloped, and the audience shrieked and children cried even when Harry finally noticed and breathed it all back in.

It was better, at least, to risk his position at the carny (for the manager was very angry until the headlines appeared) than to take it all home with him.

For Vera's first attempt had been understandably distressing. She had spent weeks bent over diagrams, constructing one series after another of valves and pumps and springs. She did it in miniature first, working on wooden dolls until successful.

She told Harry that she was ready, and she stood before him in the fifth position in her flesh-colored tights and her flexible legs, excited and pleased.

Harry turned on the music and Vera slowly moved her elegant carved limbs and bent her knee. She did a marvelous extension, and Harry appreciated the difficulty-of all that dead weight being held up by truncated muscles.

And then Vera stepped quickly and folded out her arms for a leap—and fell head forward, body heavy, head slamming the floor.

"Damn! Damn! Damn!" she cried as Harry rushed forward, his breath indrawn, "I lost the balance! Oh hell! Oh hell!" She wailed, a cracked, shattered doll on the floor, as tears flowed down Harry's cheek and a controlled sobbing shook him. He was afraid to open his mouth, to soothe or to sob.

"Give it up, Vera!" he demanded that night, and then, "Go ahead, I know you can do it!" when he saw her the next morning dressed and at the barre. She had slept deeply and immediately once he had carried her to bed; he was the one who had tossed and fretted in grief. He was terrified that she would feel failure. He stood back from her in dread for her.

Harry became increasingly friendly with R. J., who was told of Vera's devices and made suggestions. He felt real warmth for Harry's haggard strain and scientific interest in Vera's crusade.

"Cheer up, Harry! Don't take it so hard! Your Vera has guts and she's resourceful. She's got art, but craft, too. No illusions, that's what I like! No tricks masquerading as mysteries. Not like some I could name, The Great Smalldini and so forth."

"I'm afraid," Harry confessed. "I'm afraid she'll find out she can't do it." "And why can't she?" R. J. protested. "You've said she's done more already than anyone thought. Why should she stop now?" R. J. stood back from his mirror, his red nose in place. "I tried a blue nose last week; the boss didn't like it. I joined the circus for the spirit of adventure, and what do I get? Stereotypes! By the way, if you're not more careful the boss is talking about changing you into a sword-eater.

5

Last night you left a flame behind and it drifted up to the trapeze guy. He has no sense of adventure, you know; he slipped." Harry groaned.

"Didn't fall, don't worry. Just made a particular *point* about it, you understand. Ever try eating ice cream? Leaves a film in the mouth."

Vera liked hearing about R. J. and eagerly examined everything he sent her. She had worked out a shunt/valve arrangement that was successful on the legs themselves when she wasn't wearing them (she was getting better about testing before trying). She was learning to flex her muscles to impact on the exact spot of the artificial legs. Part of her exercise consisted of walking around on her stumps and pretending she had feet. This startled Harry the first time he saw it and he crashed into a chair, upsetting something. He blurted out, "Don't leave your legs lying around!" and Vera laughed in a rare instance of mockery.

Vera practiced for two weeks before admitting that the legs indeed were capable of a certain spring, but no real lift. There was no possibility of a frappé, for instance. She told this to Harry, who told it to R. J., who sent back two small pumps formerly used to inflate clowns in a special suit, before the routine was banned.

"It worked fine, though," R. J. said. "We'd sit down to a huge platter of spaghetti in the middle of the act and start inflating. Of course it was tempting to see if you could inflate just a little bit more, but the boss said popping a balloon is just popping a balloon whether there's someone in it or not."

"It exploded?"

"And me with a hole in my long johns."

Vera flushed with pleasure as she fingered R. J.'s pumps. It was six months after the accident. Vera's agent had sent her get-well cards and flowers, followed by a legal release from her contract. He valued his reputation as a humane man. Vera tore up the release and sent back a notice that she would be well enough to perform in an additional six months. The agent kept that letter on his desk, wondering how to answer it, and silently added to it another letter that set a date for her return performance. He did not have much of a sense of humor.

Harry knew all about this and encouraged her in the new voice he had adopted: supportive, caring, and hearty. He never could do it well enough to keep his eyes from shifting. He noticed that Vera seemed to have forgotten that most people had flesh-and-bone legs. In fact, she refused to believe that the wooden ones were not her natural legs. One day, for example, Harry noted that his foot had fallen asleep, and Vera replied, "It's the damp in here; the wood swells." This contrasted with other quirks: at night, she would sometimes scratch Harry's leg if she felt an imaginary itch in her own. She was losing the concept of legs as personal. Her increasing absorption in pumps and lifts and valves inclined her toward believing that any other sort of leg was a disadvantage, if not outright stupidity. Whenever she heard of an anomaly in anyone else's leg, six toes for instance, she would say without blinking, "How could anyone let that happen? I could get rid of that extra toe in ten minutes." Harry had terrible thoughts that someday she would catch her finger in a door and decide to get wooden hands. Vera had read anatomy books as she was modifying her legs, and her mind was filled with structure. The human body, piston engines, elevator shafts, pogo sticks—all animation was being tied together, all movement becoming function. She had turned, little by little, into an engineer of the dance, a designer of motion. And she still maintained a hold on her sense of the flow of ballet; she saw it simply as making substitutions, as building a new form of the art—one which acknowledged the underlying machine.

She made sure that R. J. was invited to her first performance. She had danced, by then, for Harry; but it was a cautious display. She was keeping in reserve her real accomplishments. Like a child, she wanted to startle Harry before an audience. She wanted to startle him, so she merely proved that she could still dance. Dancing well would be the surprise.

She took Stravinsky's *Firebird* as her theme, relying on her previous performances of it. She made changes as she went along.

In rehearsal she had mastered her leaps. The height she achieved now was singular. She knew her tools well, she had worked with dedication and high art in perfecting them—those legs, those instruments of motion. There were springs in her legs, and she now knew springs. There were pumps and valves and she understood their place in nature—for nature now included, almost demanded, the artificial, the imposed construction. She performed in front of a small but interested audience. She had had a reputation, and her career had been followed. The invitations were strictly confined to those who understood dance; there were no media manipulators, no curiosity seekers involved. Maybe she did not consider that her dance would have generated tabloid space. It is possible she did not; she had already forgotten life before the accident.

Harry sweated through his shirt and through his jacket. He gulped containers of milk before he left and kept all sorts of coated pills and tablets on hand. R. J., in contrast, was pleased and excited. He felt a proprietary interest in Vera's performance. He confessed to no particular interest in ballet; he wanted to see those legs. "A year of work," he said in satisfaction. "Gave her some of my best little parts. Sort of makes you think—she's got a history of my tricks there with her now. I'm not meaning to make little of it, you understand. I mean only that it's curious how a thing like a screw, for instance, can be used in one machine and then it's not needed and gets used somewhere else, and all the time, you see, that screw is sort of carrying along the history of having a place in someone else's history. You see what I mean? Vera has parts of my life with her now. Funny how you never think of it-the bits and pieces of things you pass through and pass along."

Harry didn't answer. He felt that R. J. was somehow taking credit for Vera. And he felt that he owed R. J. a lot. The two sensations worked to leave him speechless. He didn't know what to say. He sighed loudly and then inhaled the bundle of flames he produced. His discomfort was rising; he unwrapped a mint.

"It's strange," R. J. continued in a different line. "I'm not a mercenary man, but if Vera pulls this off, it's got to mean that the accident didn't ruin her career, and that must make a difference in how much damages you'd get awarded, no? I mean, just because she's enterprising doesn't mean that cornice didn't do the same amount of damage to her legs. She could have just sat in a wheelchair. You know, if she doesn't pull it off tonight, the money might come through more. Interesting. But if she does do well, who knows? She might make more money out of this than if she didn't get hurt. After all, her legs can't give out now, can they? If they do, she can just fix 'em up again."

The music began. Vera did not play with spotlights or with shadows. The stage was brilliantly lit.

She stood center stage. She did not look remarkable. The audience was alert, ready to remember any and every jerky movement, any hint of wood.

What they saw was novel, inventive, and offensive. Vera used every implement her legs possessed. If she leaped and wished to stop leaping, she had to bring her heel down flat. To make that into a step, she crouched low, like a waiting animal. There was nothing awkward in her performance—but on the other hand, no movement was finished in the usual way.

As a consequence, everyone familiar with ballet was terribly disoriented. Nothing expected happened: she neither fell nor landed properly. No one could relax.

Vera leaped and pivoted; she mimicked the new movements of her legs with bent arms that had in them the suggestion of wood. Her face was carved into a classic mask

Harry saw only that Vera was doing it—she had conquered the entrechat royale; she did not fall. He held his breath in; he longed for the open air. The audience was uneasy. The critics were already having difficulty about whether or not they should review Vera. She had made it into a technical performance—a tour de force of some kind, surely, but could this strangely mechanical dance be called a ballet? Wasn't her frappe more like a demonstration than an ecstatic flow?

And those leaps! Whatever could one say about them? How could any one human rise so high? Wasn't that a contrivance? And wasn't contrivance opposed to the soul of the art? Trained eyes dived to the floor when she leaped: What gave that trampoline effect? Untrained eyes glanced upward: Were there wires?

Harry heard the muttering behind him.

"A trick of some kind."

"A display, not a performance."

"A mockery. It's obscene."

"Could *you* do that without legs?" Harry hissed.

"The question is: Could you do it *with* legs?"

In the middle of Vera's most spectacular leap (reports cited it as fully five feet in the air), Harry belched fire. He was facing Vera, in the front row. The flames spat out like a torch and wrapped around her ankles.

"Another trick?" was whispered uncertainly.

"An effect; it's like a movie."

But it was not an effect. As Vera came down, the fire was sucked into the valves in her feet; her slippers lit up, her toes began to smoke.

She cast an anguished glance at Harry, who was sucking in air like a brother in a Chinese folktale. But it was too late. The fire had hold of Vera's cherished feet. She danced faster and faster; she was lighter than ever. Her burning feet frapped wildly. Her body spun her legs around—a flaming arabesque, a blinding promenade. She flew, she positively flew along with the fire, feeding it, making it a partner. People began to rise and groan with fear and pity: "Oh, do something, someone, please!"

Harry inhaled all he could, then he breathed out, rushing forward with renewed fire. For a second the stage was lit with intense brightness; then all was quiet. The fire was out.

Vera knelt on one knee center stage. Her arms were gracefully crossed on her breast. Her burnt leg was under her. The music was done. Her heart raced in triumph.

"Horrible, horrible," a critic whimpered. "A travesty, it was all deliberate. She was never in danger."

The rumor spread throughout the auditorium: The fire was part of the performance. Stunning, but manipulative. "She figured it all out herself," R. J. chuckled to his neighbor. "I never told her about that. Of course they wouldn't let me do anything like that in the carny; might cause panic, they'd say. Of course, if it was billed that way, say, the magnificent burning ballerina, then people would expect it and they'd be able to appreciate it. That's what the carny is *for.*"

Enough people heard him for the phrase to be part of three reviews that night. "Where does ballet end and the circus begin?" began one writer. "We all found out tonight. However startling the performance was, however admirable the effort that went into this rehabilitation, the end result was not art, but artifice; not a dance, but a show. All you ringmasters out there, take note."

I, Harry's boss read the article and approached Vera and Harry.

"You can do anything you want," he reasoned, "as long as you burn up at the end. I'll pay you a good salary, a very good salary. Millions of people will see you. Consider that."

"Never!" Harry cried, his arm around Vera.

"Don't be crazy, Harry. Let's hear what Vera says."

She was calmly working on a new leg. "I am a dancer," she said. "With wooden legs. It's a new art."

"You don't belong in the circus," Harry insisted.

"They'll never let me perform on a stage again. The insurance alone.... Let me think."

"Rub the legs in alcohol," R. J. said. "They'll bum blue."

"I could do anything I wanted, then," Vera said. "No restrictions."

"Is it what you want?" Harry was amazed.

"You could make your fire animals leap along with her," R. J. added.

"It would make an interesting *Swan Lake*," Vera smiled.

"This is no joke, Vera."

"Oh, but Harry," she answered quietly. "Harry, it is."

The Other Door

Ione was almost completely finished cleaning her tiny apartment. The main room had a kitchenette along one wall and a sofa, a coffee table, an armchair, and a bookcase in the living area. This took half an hour to straighten out. The second room had a bed, a night table, and a bureau. If she'd had more furniture, she would have felt cramped, but she was poor and that's all there was. She was grateful for these gloomy rooms, and she had enough around her to provide comfort if not luxury. Ione was well aware that wealth existed, but she knew there was also destitution. She was poised on an edge somewhere on the lower end of the scale, but she did not know want, and that was a blessing.

She hadn't planned on cleaning the closet, but since it was going so well she decided to check. It was tidy and half-empty; she didn't have many clothes. She gave a quick glance around the room and noticed—it was one of those things that one simply stopped noticing after a while—the other door that was blocked by the bureau. It led to a closet that was really too shallow to be of much use, so she had simply abandoned it.

But, really, she hadn't looked inside for years now. It's impossible to ignore things for so long, to go on forever without at least a cursory check.

She pushed the bureau aside and opened the door.

Well, how very strange. It was a room.

It was actually a beautiful room, even though it was empty. It was twice the size of her apartment and had high ceilings and long, elegant windows. There were trees outside the windows, and Ione couldn't imagine exactly where they were growing—some area in back of the building must have gardens.

She was surprised at herself. Why, with a room like this in her apartment—why would she choose to squeeze herself into the area she now lived in? It's true that she didn't require much, but this was obviously an extraordinary asset. She went to the windows. Well, they would need cleaning; they would certainly need cleaning. She rubbed a circle in the glass to get a better view. There was, indeed, a beautiful garden out there, green and leafy with low stone walls and a garden walk. The trees next to the window were lacy and elegant; the trunks were narrow and the branches didn't block the sun. A pattern of light and shadow flickered beautifully; she could even feel patches of sun on her face. How could she possibly have forgotten this room?

There was plaster molding along the walls and around the original, unpainted window frames. There were built-in nooks and drawers and cabinets, and none of the floorboards squeaked. In fact, the boards were hardwood with a reddish cast; they would clean up very well.

Ione, standing in the middle of the room with her lips pursed and her head held slightly to the side, decided that she would start moving her furniture over immediately, just as soon as she washed the floor and all the windows. Perhaps that's why she had ignored the room all these years—it certainly was large and it would take longer to clean than she was used to. Over the next few days she cleaned and polished the room so that it glowed; she moved her furniture through the doorway and found an old bolt of gauzy material in a little built-in cupboard in the room; she used it to make beautifully delicate curtains. After a while she passed through her old apartment as if it were a foyer; she couldn't believe she had really lived there.

Although she had very little furniture, she liked the simplicity of her huge room. She occasionally found little items in the drawers in the cabinets and cupboards; there always seemed to be a drawer she'd over looked. One day she finally finished putting paper in all the drawers and hanging all her clothes in the clothes closet, her brooms and mops in the broom closet. She went to the door at the far side of the room, which she assumed was a linen closet.

When she opened it, however, there were further surprises.

She saw a hallway. Did this door lead out of the apartment—a second entrance that she had neglected, all these years, by never looking at it?

It was a rather wide hallway, though, and it had a grand piano in it. Ione played a few bars of a piece she'd learned to play some twenty years ago, when she was a child taking lessons. The piano was perfectly in tune. She thought, "Why did I stop taking lessons? I've always loved to play. As long as this piano is here (and if no one minds) why, I can play to my heart's content. I can study again; I feel happier just thinking about it."

The hallway, instead of being an exit, led to another door.

And there Ione hesitated. She looked back over her shoulder to the dimly lit hallway. In fact, it seemed more like a long ballroom of some kind than any hallway she'd ever seen. "Yes, a gallery!" she thought as the word leaped to mind. There was a beautiful carpet patterned in trellises and roses; there was that piano and the overall feel of the room with its lack of tenants' doorways and its lack of stairs.

It was ridiculous how she used to live, considering how large her apartment truly was. This gallery, too, must be part of her apartment, or else there would be a stairway here instead of a door. This door must lead out to the hallway she'd been expecting.

Ione opened the door and blinked.

The room was well lit and there were people in it.

She was just about to back out and pull the door shut again when a voice called out, quite happily: "Ione!"

The voice stopped Ione dead in her tracks. It was familiar.

"Ione! It's me, Elizabeth!" The woman came toward her, arms out spread.

Well, it was an extraordinary thing that Ione hadn't even thought of Elizabeth for years, but the sight of her—oh, the sight of her!—quickened her heart.

"You're back!" Elizabeth cried.

"Oh, how lonely I've been without you!" As soon as Ione said it, she realized it was true. To see her friend again, to find the loss that (it was true) had made her life feel barren and pale; how was it possible to have neglected her so long?

"Ah, now that you're here we'll all be happy again!" Elizabeth cried.

"All? Who do you mean by 'all'?"

And from the doorway behind Elizabeth's shoulder, another beloved face came forward, and the sight of him made Ione cry out in a pain so piercing and dizzying that she staggered on her feet and whispered, "Daniel!"

Like a traveler stepping off the train to a busy station, like a patient waking from a fevered sleep, like a reader released from a heart-rending tale, she had left them. She had lived otherwise; but she was now home. She fell into his arms and no arms had ever seemed so comforting; she looked up and saw the faces of people she had loved the most in life, standing and smiling at her in rooms bathed in golden light, eager to see her, speak to her, crying out gaily on their luck, their happiness, the completeness of their lives.

The light surrounding all of them was extraordinary, a light that radiated from lamps and chandeliers and, it seemed, even from their hearts, their lips. It made the wonder and happiness and homecoming seem to last in an uninterrupted, extended feeling of love. "How could I have left them; how could I have forgotten?" she wondered only on the first day. After that there were no questions; there was simply happiness and joy.

At night they danced to old records, or read to each other, or played card games with rules they made up on the spot. It was on one of those nights, as Ione got up to get a glass of wine, that she passed a door in the hallway leading to the kitchen.

She stopped and looked back down the hall, to where those she loved leaned close to one another, laughing and spirited, in the glow of a lamp. They composed a vivid oval of warmth and invitation.

Ione turned slowly to the door and opened it.

There was a staircase made of rocks set tight together, winding down ward and out of sight. But even though she couldn't see where it led, Ione could hear the sounds of an orchestra playing a waltz. Strauss, was it? Some waltz she recognized, although the name escaped her. It was beautiful music, her favorite in fact; she hadn't heard it in years and she'd forgotten all about it.

It was a revelation to hear such music again.

Ione closed the door behind her and descended the stairs.

16

Deep Green

Rafel started hunting somewhat late in life, but he must have been born with a taste for blood because, once started, he was always on the lookout for things to kill. As far as CarolAnn was concerned, you put a gun in a man's hand and he immediately thinks he's God. She'd seen, throughout her life, close to a hundred Gods, a lot of them in bars with trophy smirks on their faces, guts hanging over their belts, and a religious conviction of their right to sporting deaths.

To CarolAnn they were beneath contempt, and she never thought she'd end up married to one. How, exactly, had Rafel managed to camouflage himself over the years? Or was it something, like baldness, that came to different men at different times? She was twenty-three, he was twenty-four, and they'd known each other four years, having met at a summer dance in college. After all, she told herself sharply in defense, before he was a hunter, he'd been the kind of man who looked up at the stars and liked to name them.

"Why are you going hunting again?" she asked for the third time.

"It's hard to explain," he said, taking the bullets out of the box, clickclick, snapping the chambers shut. "It's almost spiritual. Private."

"Spiritual," she huffed. "Blowing out brains if you're a good shot. Shooting off ears or eyes or toes if you're not."

"Women don't understand." He said it calmly and stood up. He wore a red plaid jacket and a red cap. He took the sandwich off the counter and stuffed it in his pocket, walked to the fridge and leaned into it, pulling out a six-pack.

"Helps you pray?" she scoffed.

"That's right," he said. "Every ritual's got something throwaway." He grinned at her. "Don't worry, honey, I think about you all the time." A horn yelped outside and Rafel lunged out the door, letting it slam behind him.

It's those friends of his, CarolAnn thought. Bad company. A bunch of five burping, big-bellied, plaid-shirted men, backslapping and trigger hungry. All with sunburns on their left arms from patrolling the world in their pickup trucks.

Sometimes you wanted to be with people who shut up and sometimes you wanted to be with people who were talkers, but CarolAnn couldn't imagine a time when she'd want to be belting down beers with a group of old boys like that.

CarolAnn and Rafel lived outside of town on a dirt road that eventually circled back into town. Lesser roads crossed this one and dribbled into the woods or to even more isolated houses. Rafel vowed that someday they'd live in town. CarolAnn assumed that was just talk; she liked where she was. Early that spring, for instance, she'd taken a branch off the dirt road that led through the woods and ended up at a log cabin ("A log cabin," she had thought with satisfaction) in a natural clearing.

And in the clearing was a vigorous woman tending her plants and roots.

"Just call me Ivy, dear," the woman said. "Ivy Stiles."

Ivy had dark brown hair the color of wet trees and eyes the color of leaves. She wore dresses in bright floral patterns-huge fronds entwined with poppies, intricate vines spilling around toothed fems, and one that CarolAnn especially liked with all kinds of buds almost bursting to open. "This is an old-fashioned garden," Ivy said with satisfaction. "Old spotted trefoil, lungwort, bladderwort, spiderwort. Henbane, Nathan's balm, love-in-a-pocket, chokecherry, foxglove, please-your-maker." She beamed at CarolAnn, hands on her hips.

"I haven't heard of all of them," CarolAnn admitted. "But some of them-they're medicinal, aren't they?"

"Herbal," Ivy said, stooping to pinch a leaf, sniffing it with pleasure. "Lore of the ages. Wisdom over the years. Trial and error, and so much of it lost already. Poultice, infusion, potion, liniment; root, leaf, seed, or twig." She bent down and pulled out a weed, tamping the soil back down again. "I happen to believe there's a cure for everything, growing right now on the earth. And not in a test tube, either, or behind lead shields. In the air, in the open, in sunshine and shade, there for the asking!" She stretched over to a bucket of water, dipped in a cup, and then spilled it around one plant in particular. "You've got to know your proper moments." She pulled the tendril of a vine running across latticework near the cabin and tucked it expertly into a groove.

"Ah, what a beautiful day," she said, squinting at the sun. "So hard to get days right. Either too hot, too cold, too wet, too dry. Good for some things, bad for others. No matter what you get, one thing dies, another lives. Cycles. Endless cycles." She cheered up. "This is a favorite of mine." She walked quickly to the end of the row and opened a small burlap bag on the ground. She motioned to CarolAnn. "Go ahead. Dig in. Quite nice." And she grabbed handfuls of seeds, looked around alertly, the tip of her tongue just protruding slightly, and then tossed it all in the air as a quick breeze carried it all away.

"Now you!" she laughed, and CarolAnn did it too, catching a breeze. Some seeds caught in her hair.

"There was a wind, once," Ivy said speculatively, "took them all the way to Oregon."

CarolAnn didn't have a chance to ask how she knew this was true, because right then a raven swooped down from the sky, landed facing Ivy, and dropped a worm at her feet.

"Very nice," Ivy beamed.

The bird gave a harsh, intricate call. It sounded like a sentence.

"In English," Ivy demanded.

The raven cocked its head sideways, giving CarolAnn a bright, hard stare.

"Visitor," it said sharply.

"Quite right. Bound to be a good friend someday. And thank you for the lovely present. Can I get you anything?"

The bird hopped impatiently from one foot to the other. "Root beer, straight up. Piece of worm on the side."

"Nonsense," Ivy said. "You gave *me* the worm."

With that the bird squawked loud and long, jumping up and down and finally flying off in anger.

"He has good intentions," Ivy said, "but what a temper!"

"He brings you worms?"

Ivy picked up her trowel and began loosening the soil at the end of the row. "Oh yes. Half for him, half for me. He offered to do it, actually, but for some reason it still drives him mad."

"And what do you do with the worms?"

Ivy looked at her in surprise. "Why, they're for the garden, of course."

"Of course."

Ivy looked at the sky. "Time for you to run along, dear. Come again soon."

CarolAnn had been wondering if she should go and was relieved that the woman understood this—unless, of course, CarolAnn was actually in the way and the woman wanted her to go.

"Next week would be pleasant," Ivy said, waving to her with the clippers she'd just picked up.

"Till then," CarolAnn said faintly. She thought about the woman all the way home and realized that she was envious. What a garden! What health and vitality! And a trained raven! "Maybe," she thought, "I could help her. I love gardening. And I bet she knows a lot.'

She was actually almost singing when she got home, she was so enthralled with the idea of the garden. CarolAnn usually grew corn and tomatoes and the like, with a small patch of dill and basil and thyme. This would be an eye-opener. "Please-your-maker," she thought happily, "love-in-a-pocket!"

As she turned the road to her own yard she saw that Rafel was home. He had the door to the garage open and the hood of his truck up. He was whistling.

"Rafe!" she called.

"Yo-ho!" he yelled, twisting himself around but still under the hood

"I had a wonderful day," she said happily. "I found a log cabin in the woods and the woman who lives there has an old-fashioned herb garden."

He came up from the engine, grinning and wiping his hands on a rag. "A gingerbread house? Was it a gingerbread house?"

She laughed. "Wrong fairy tale."

He loped over to her, hanging an arm over her shoulder. "I had a good day too," he said.

She stiffened and looked into his face, waiting.

"Come with me," he crooned, walking around the house with her under his arm, "to the Magic Kingdom." He stopped and grinned happily. "The Horn of Plenty. Paradise. Down this aisle to your produce section."

"You killed something," she said.

"Uh-huh. Bonus day. I killed a few somethings."

She set her mouth grimly and followed him to the back porch. There, in a heap, were two rabbits, a squirrel, and a duck. "The squirrel was just for fun," he said. "We're not hillbillies."

"They're bleeding on the floor."

"Think of it as gravy," he laughed.

"I can't eat them," she said, turning away.

"The guys say all the wives get squeamish," Rafel laughed, "until they get hungry."

"Not me. I won't do it."

"You'll come 'round," he said stoically. "It's kinda cute. I'll skin them for you."

"For me?" she repeated in a small voice.

"And what kind of work does this hunter of yours do?" Ivy asked weeks later, when CarolAnn was in the firm habit of confiding everything to her. "He's a builder," she said unhappily. "I used to think that was romantic, but I've seen how builders work. They make the land flat and bare. They cut down the trees, they bulldoze the hills. There are no slopes left, only men sitting on power mowers on Saturday, going back and forth on their lawns."

"Nasty," Ivy agreed. She was turning over one of the compost piles. "Tires the eye." She frowned. "What will he do once he gets rid of all the trees? They need trees to build the houses, don't they? They'll keep going till it's all the same and flat and no shade in sight."

"There's a stand of pine—oh, they must be 100 feet tall or more—on one of the paths coming here," CarolAnn said. "You can't see the sky there, but it's so quiet and the light takes a long time drifting down. And it's so tall I feel like a child every time, but a very calm, wise child. I'm even grateful that I don't matter, compared to those trees."

"People who don't know the woods become unnatural. Machines maybe, not animals."

"That's it," CarolAnn said, "that's Rafel. Lost the belief in life, in living things." She stooped down beside Ivy, pulling out weeds around the aloe.

"Not that," Ivy said quickly. "That's dandelion. I like it."

"Sorry." She bit her lip for a moment. "What bothers me—and I hope you don't mind if I speak frankly—"

"Never. I never mind frankness."

"Well. I worry, you see, that I might get pregnant. I wouldn't mind if I could be sure it would be my child, but what if it's his?" She lowered her voice. "It's such a struggle now, you see, because he's impulsive, he never waits, and I think of him peeling the skin off those animals, so they look naked and wet like newborns. It frightens me."

"Tsk," Ivy said. "That's not right. Men are meant for making love, aren't they? If you don't want children, it's as easy as pie. There's a vine over there," she gestured past the end of the plantings, "that I guarantee will take care of it. Snip off a bit and plant it outside your bedroom window."

"As easy as that?" CarolAnn asked, surprised.

"Well, easy, yes, once you get it. I suppose it depends how you feel about wells."

"Wells," CarolAnn repeated speculatively.

"They always *are* down wells," Ivy said, "these particular vines. They're just hard to get at, it's a sort of passage rite. Down the well, eh? Makes you think. Why not on a mountain or the end of a very long road or even off the side of a cliff? But it's a well," she said, pinching off the blooms of the marigold. "It's always a well."

"That's all right," CarolAnn said faintly. "I've never been *in* a well. But I think it will be all right."

Ivy squinted up to the sky. "Sun's high. Of course it won't matter, but it's all psychology. Come along with me."

And they set off at a very swift pace, trotting almost, and CarolAnn was astonished as they passed a field of red poppies. "Poppies, eh?" Ivy trilled. "All quiet here, get it? What a beautiful bloom! Don't sniff!" And Ivy snorted in her cheery way, so that CarolAnn wasn't sure if there was more to the joke than she imagined.

They came to an old stone well with a wooden crank, and a rope with a wooden bucket. There was blue cohosh, black cohosh, motherwort, and false unicorn growing around it. CarolAnn could recognize these by now and she knew they were useful aids for pregnancy and childbirth.

22

CarolAnn peered over the edge, down the rock-contoured sides of the well, down to the darkness. She felt a coolness rise up to meet her, coolness and dark.

"It's best if you crank the bucket all the way down, and then hold the rope and climb down the wall. It's much easier than it seems." Ivy seemed noncommittal.

"And the vine?"

"You'll recognize it."

She rolled down the bucket till it rested on the water, then she raised it slightly and tied the rope off at that point.

Although she'd never done anything like it before, she found that one foothold after another was in place, that the rope had irregularities that made it easier to hold on to as well as move down, and that once she moved into the darkness, she found a natural, effortless rhythm. In fact, she felt strong. By the time she reached the bucket (surprisingly fast, she thought) her eyes were just beginning to adjust to the dark; she could almost make out the shapes of the larger rocks in the walls.

As she sat yoga-style on the bucket, her eyes began to see more and more, and indeed there was a pale iridescent light coming from behind her, and when she turned to look she saw the vine glowing along the edge of the black water. She could feel the dampness rising, the cold rising from beneath the bucket, and she rubbed her arms.

"Are you all right, dear?" Ivy's voice drifted toward her from far, far above, only as loud as a whisper, making CarolAnn wonder if she'd actually heard it.

"Yes," was all she answered, and because of the closeness of the walls, the sibilant "s" whispered on, sighing, or so she thought. "Yes oh yes oh yes," twisted around her and finally died away.

CarolAnn narrowed her eyes, squinting at shapes in the darkness. The vine had a steady phosphorescent light, always just too dim to make things out firmly, but then she saw a few of the glowing leaves dance, and she leaned out over her bucket and squinted harder.

She blinked and rubbed her eyes. A branch seemed to be swaying right in front of her, until her eyes adjusted even further and she could tell it was a snake, and it was singing, almost under its breath.

CarolAnn froze.

"Oh yes, so swift, so soft, so shy," it sang;

I saw a shadow, just a shadow
What's this?
What's this?
Some shadow searching for me?
Oh yes, so swift, I knew the shape.
It's his, it's his, it's his.

And the snake hummed slightly, bobbing its head agreeably.

CarolAnn felt oddly objective about her own fear. The snake showed no hostility; in fact, its song was slightly dreamlike, its movements somewhat hypnotic. There was no reason to be alarmed, as long as it simply swayed and fluted its fluttering tongue.

However, the snake was wrapped all through the vine and so CarolAnn reached forward slowly; she had to go past it to get a cutting. The snake nodded and followed her hand as she neared the wall. Her fingers touched its skin—cold and springy, curiously comforting—and the snake hissed gently, turning its head and resting it on her hand. It seemed to watch her adoringly. She twisted her hand and began to feel her way along the vine for a healthy section loosely rooted to the wall.

"It's his, it's his, it's his," the snake sang and began to trail slowly up her arm, coiling around and around as CarolAnn followed one promising branch and pulled it gently away from its crevice.

She felt the snake's breath as it reached her face and nuzzled her hair. Its tail was just leaving her wrist, following its coil up her arm. "Oh yes, oh yes, oh yes," it sang.

Her own movements by now were almost imperceptible. She was uncertain what the snake would do, so intimately coiled around her, but she had her goal now, she had the vine. There was no point in waiting quietly, hoping the snake would move on. It hummed gently in her ear, "What's this? What's this?" It was reassuring and ominous at the same time, and even charming. It was hard not to wait around to find out what would happen, or whether its song would ever change.

"Some shadow searching for me?" it hummed as she raised her hand up slowly and grabbed the rope. It seemed to make itself comfortable around her shoulders and she raised the other arm, hoisting herself up slowly to stand on the bucket. She began to inch her way up carefully, and as she moved the snake began to curve from her neck

24

down her back to her waist. By the time she was halfway up, it was coiling down her leg, singing faintly, regretfully.

It left her foot and slithered along the rope, slipping downward, still trailing sibilants.

By the time CarolAnn reached sunshine her heart was hammering and an overwhelming terror threatened to engulf her. She listened as the snake slid into the water, but she was afraid if she looked back she would see it turn and follow her. It was strange that she was only afraid after the snake left.

She was frantic to see Ivy; she propelled herself up and over the well with a wild eye, looking for the herb woman. She crawled over onto the ground, the vine in her right hand, panting. She was alone.

She rolled over onto her feet when a large bird flew over her head, cawing. She stumbled after it, until she found Ivy. The woman was unconcernedly pulling off comfrey leaves and putting them on racks to dry. She was surrounded by racks.

CarolAnn was speechless when she reached her; it seemed impossible to express her fear, outrage, mistrust. Why had Ivy walked away? Was indifference justified? Had it really not mattered?

She stood open-mouthed in front of her. Ivy turned and smiled.

The raven swooped down from overhead, landing between CarolAnn and the herb woman. It laid its worm down on the ground and hopped anxiously, peering first at one woman, then another.

"Made it back, made it back," it shouted.

"Of course," Ivy said, undisturbed. "You always do. What a lovely worm. What can I get you?"

The bird hooted and peered at her craftily. "Comfrey? Comfrey tea?"

"Oh, you can see it's not ready. It takes days to dry." She turned away.

"My worm," the raven said, picking it up again.

Ivy frowned, not answering.

"Your worm," the bird said, and laid it at CarolAnn's feet.

Ivy looked up and smiled. "So much nicer than a snake, isn't it? The raven must like you." She went back to her leaves and her rack.

CarolAnn picked up the worm without a word and headed home. She planted the vine outside her bedroom window and patted the worm in with it.

That night she felt free of moral qualms as she lay with Rafel. She slept late and he was gone in the morning.

She tended her own garden first. It was meager because so much blood had ruined the soil, and most of the ground remained stubbornly bare.

She heard the swoosh of the raven's wings first and sat up from her weeding, shielding her eyes from the sun.

"Tired of worms," the raven said, bobbing its head and dipping it to leave a present at her feet.

"A newt," she said, cradling it in her hand. "Red-spotted newt. I've always liked them."

The newt curled itself quietly, a small cool touch in her hand, almost weightless. She blew air on it and it turned its head.

"Thank you very much," she said politely.

"Not at all," the bird croaked and hopped up to the nearest branch. It ruffed out its throat feathers, shaking back and forth on its legs.

"Dancing," CarolAnn remarked.

"Please do," it answered, and she was amused to think it actually wanted her to dance. She placed the newt carefully in her pocket and lifted her arms to match the raven's flapping wings when a gun went off very close, and the raven yelled and was gone.

She spun around and saw Rafel.

"My aim could have been better," he grinned, "but you were so close."

"Why do you have to keep killing?" she demanded, trembling.

"Don't be silly," he said, hooking his arm over her shoulder and leading her inside. "I missed!"

He whistled and she clenched her teeth. When he opened the door to the kitchen she saw that he had arranged his last set of kills around the table, propped up on chairs, leaning their heads onto plates, slack-jawed, glassy-eyed. He had pots on the stove with animals leaning out of them, their paws on the rims.

She stood there, dizzy. "You never used to be this way," she cried.

"I'm just honest, is all. This country life agrees with me. It's kill or be killed, dog-eat-dog. I salute the food chain." He curled a raccoon's fingers around a fork and mimicked him eating.

"Stop it!"

"Bleeding heart," he snapped. "Can't you see you're pretending? You can't live without killing, no one can."

"For sport?" she cried. "For fun?"

"I am the provider."

She ran out the door and down the road into the forest. "Which one of us has changed?" she cried.

She took an unfamiliar path that led along a stream and through a tall, silent forest with brown pine needles muffling her steps. She was surprised to see Ivy when she reached a thinner patch of trees. The herb woman was bobbing and humming, pulling saplings out of a cloth bag strung over her shoulder and planting them quickly. CarolAnn turned away without speaking and continued until she came onto a clearing. It was a hot day and still, and when she saw the pond she went toward it, splashing water on her face.

She sat back and took out the newt, putting it carefully on the ground near a small puddle of water. It opened its mouth, leaning forward, as if trying to drink but unable to.

CarolAnn opened the salamander's mouth carefully with a twig. A small red object, about the size of a raspberry, fell onto the ground. It was beating.

She looked at it, puzzled, then picked it up and held it. Gradually she realized that it was beating almost exactly the same as her own pulse.

"It's a heart," she thought suddenly.

She rolled it slowly across her palm. She could see it pump in and out.

She heard the swoosh, and closed her palm to guard against the breeze of the raven's wings.

The bird hopped closer. "Rafel's heart," it said distinctly.

"No," she said, suddenly afraid. "Surely it's too small to be a man's heart?"

"Rafel's heart," it repeated emphatically.

She lowered her head and considered. It was true, Rafe had changed dramatically. It was true, he had lost the edge of kindness—so much so that she dreaded seeing him. But she had hoped it would pass. She lifted her head. "Raven, are you sure this is Rafel's heart?"

The bird spread its wings and lifted them over its head. "I saw it. Popped out of his mouth, but he didn't notice. Took it myself."

She nodded. "Gave it to newt."

Her head sank back down, and she fell into a gloom as she thought of Rafel before he'd lost his heart. It was easy to see now that that was exactly what had happened.

Even her hands sank down as the gloom settled over her, still holding Rafel's raspberry heart. "I remember how once I loved him," she thought, and she had to close her eyes. That day passed, and then the night passed, and CarolAnn still sat there, the heart in her hand pulsing, her chin upon her chest.

Morning came, and she didn't notice it, and the sun warmed her skin and then warmed it some more. She licked her lips once, and they were still dry.

The raven lifted into the sky, between CarolAnn and the sun, so his shadow fell on her, and he was joined by one raven after another, so that the birds lifted up from the ground in tiers by the hundreds, flowing up like a mirrored waterfall, the tips of their wings never touching, their beaks spread wide.

It was the whooshing and calling that woke her finally, in the shadow of all those wings. She blinked, trying to swallow.

"Drink this, dear," Ivy said, and offered her a mix of valerian and rue. "I do like herbs. I like greens, they never need to deviate. It's the shock, rue's always good for shock. I learned it when I was a child. What's that you have in your hand?"

"Rafel's heart," CarolAnn whispered, showing it to her.

"That's what it looked like to me," Ivy said kindly. "Salamanders, you know, never speak. But they eat secrets. I always look under their tongues, first thing, when there's a mystery."

"What'll I do with his heart?" CarolAnn asked.

"To keep it alive," Ivy said neutrally, "you have to keep it under your tongue."

She waited politely until CarolAnn lifted her hand up to her mouth. The heart fit snugly under her tongue, beating like an extra artery.

The last of the birds flew away. CarolAnn felt revived. "I am stronger than all this," she said.

Ivy smiled. "Yes. You are."

"And I will keep this heart under my tongue, like a secret."

"A secret," the raven cried.

"I believe he's got a crush on you," Ivy laughed.

"And I'll have two hearts beating," CarolAnn said dreamily, "wherever I go. More than enough. A heart to spare."

She smiled at the bird and then turned to Ivy. She found it easy to keep the heart in place when she spoke. "And what should I do with this heart?"

"It's yours now, you know, to keep or to give away."

The two leaned back on their heels. "I could keep it," CarolAnn said. "It's good to have so much bounty. To feel so much hope, such excess." She smiled.

"And is that what you'll do? Keep it all to yourself?"

CarolAnn smiled again, because she was thinking. That night she went back home, and she stepped over the bones of Rafe's latest feast. She fed him brandy, and while he slept she kissed him and slipped his heart back under his tongue. Every morning when he woke she checked his heart, and every evening, too. When it seemed too weak she ground up foxglove and hawthorn; when it seemed erratic she tried borage or angelica. He left his gun behind the door and studied the stars again.

After a while CarolAnn pulled out the vine by the bedroom window. She needed Rafe's help with this because the vine had gone through a chink in the foundation and spread through the walls and ceiling to surround the room. They couldn't get at it all, but it was obviously the root that mattered, because CarolAnn conceived a child.

She gave birth to a beautiful girl with a beautiful heart. CarolAnn could see it beating under the pale thin skin, and it was a large heart already, larger than Rafe's, too big to hide under a salamander's tongue, firmly in place and beating like thunder.

The Hole Story

The hole suddenly appeared early one Monday morning in the middle of Main Street in Springer.

The first car skidded to a terrified halt and backed its way carefully out. Traffic was not officially rerouted until noontime. It took that long for the various phone calls to reach the various officials.

The officials of Springer had to be persuaded to come out and look. They were commandeered by the local news reporter, who knew where they ate lunch.

The head of the Department of Roads admitted it was a very large hole. "Too big to be considered a pothole," he said, "officially."

"What is it then?" asked the supervisor of Traffic and Transportation.

"A hole, of course," said Roads. "I think it might be a sewer."

Sewers's office was notified, but he had called in sick. Meanwhile traffic went elsewhere and people came out to look at the hole.

On Tuesday Laura Wilcox came up to a policeman standing by the barrier around the hole and claimed it had swallowed her husband.

"He went out for a walk last night and never came back," she said. "But you can see the bottom of the hole," the officer pointed out. Laura peered over the edge. She admitted there was nothing down there. "Nothing?" someone asked. "My daughter's bike rolled down there this morning. Can't you see it?"

The officer looked down and shrugged. "Someone must have climbed down and gotten it."

No one could prove that either way, and out of curiosity people began to throw large objects down late at night, after the police left.

Roads, on being again approached about the hole, flippantly said, "Make it into a swimming hole," and the idea took everyone's fancy (it was a very hot summer). That night people ran their hoses out to the hole and turned on the water, lowering the pressure for the entire town and annoying the Springer Fire Department.

"That hole's a nuisance and a danger," said Fire. "Where's the mayor?"

"Unavailable for comment," said Roads. "Bribery charges."

"We have to call someone in about this."

Roads sighed and got on the phone. He called in a contractor, who whistled in delight and said, "Twenty truckloads of fill and a ton of stabilizer. A beauty of a hole."

"Just fill it," Roads said. "I'll sign."

The contractor got on the phone and all the next day trucks backed into Main Street, lifted their loads and spilled them into the hole. Children adored it.

By nightfall the hole was still there and the contractor was sweating. "I estimated wrong," he said. "Not twenty truckloads. It must be a sinkhole of some kind."

"A sinkhole?"

"Everything you put in it just sinks out of sight."

"Then you can't fill it," Roads said. "And, logically, you haven't filled it with your dirt."

"I brought in twenty truckloads of fill and a ton of stabilizer."

"Yes, but where did you *put* them? The contract clearly stated that you were to use them to fill the hole."

"But I did!"

"No," Roads said sadly, "you may have put it *in* the hole, but it hasn't done anything about filling it. Breach of contract." He sighed in sympathy. "I'm sorry, but I'm an elected official. And you know what voters are like."

"I'll sue," the contractor said.

"Go ahead." Roads was unperturbed. He called in surveyors to measure the hole daily, and satisfied everyone that it was neither increasing nor decreasing. There was no danger that the whole town would proceed listlessly down its depths, as the dirt had.

"A natural monument?" the Department of Tourism murmured wistfully. "Could we leave it alone and declare it a Site?"

"If you declare it a Site, you'll have to insure it," the adjuster said.

"I'm already over budget."

"A Site must be insured."

"It isn't a Site," agreed Tourism sadly.

"Then it must be a Hazard. If it's not a Site."

"Don't hazards have to be insured?"

"Not if they're natural. If they're an act of God, they can't be." The adjuster looked around the table. "Is there anyone here who can prove this isn't an act of God?"

"We need consultants; we need reports," someone murmured. "I never do anything without a report."

"We have Roads's report. We have the surveyor's report. And the contractor's."

"But they're all so inconclusive."

The adjuster pondered. "We don't know the specialty," he admitted. "There's no sense in going the usual channels," Roads advised. "I've tried that. We can either declare the whole thing deliberate, and build a bridge, or try to get to the bottom of it."

The adjuster snickered. "The bottom of it, eh?"

"Entirely unintentional." But Taxes winked at Utilities, and a subdued, sly levity spread out among them; their eyes gleamed.

"He said 'the hole thing' too, didn't he?" Tourism pointed out. "Maybe this is all a pun," Roads said. "Maybe we should get a semanticist."

"I think we need a physicist. It might be a black hole," said Transportation.

The adjuster snickered. "I don't think it's a physical hole at all. I think it's an analogy, like Plato's cave."

"I hope it's not an analogy."

"It could be a meteorite hole. A geologist would know." They continued to ponder.

Meanwhile, Laura's husband, George, was approaching the matter from a different perspective. He had, it is true, gone for a walk after slamming the door hard on his way out. It had been a standard argument, ending in a standard way—a crescendo of words punctuated by a wooden bang. George was on his way to the only bar in town when he passed the hole and stopped, hands in his pockets, idly counting pennies and dimes. He dipped back on his heels, whistling tunelessly, determined *not* to be a man maddened by an argument. He dipped forward, leaning slightly over the edge, thinking.

And fell in.

He fell into the hole and was swallowed, like water swallows a diver. He tried to fling his arms out, and his arms stayed by his side. He twisted and fell faster and faster, and though he tried, he could find no air and in a space of time that seemed neither long nor short, his world went black and he continued to fall, without resistance.

When he awoke the sun was setting again. He stood up, started to brush himself off, and began to look around.

He was in a garbage dump, at the very top of the highest heap of garbage he had ever seen, an unending, relentless mass, an incredible terrain.

"I've hit my head," he thought. "I've hurt my eyes, my brain, I'm lost forever. That bitch."

He saw figures moving over the mounds of garbage. Two were coming to him, waving their arms and shouting. George squinted, wondering what to do. He turned around but what little light was left showed only the same unyielding landscape, hill and valley, of trash.

The two figures scrambled closer. George backed off and fell over a pile of discarded spray cans. The two figures leaned over him anxiously and silently. George blinked in resentment. "What is it?" he barked. "You never seen anyone like me before?" His specialty was anger; he broke out in it whenever he felt uncomfortable or uncertain. It convinced everyone but Laura.

The strangers were dressed in filthy rags and different varieties of cast offs. They stared at him blankly, their mouths open. Their breath stank.

George tried to scramble backward—he had no intentions of staying with these two—when a strange vehicle, patched and misshapen, came over the next slope and aimed itself at George, pulling up short with a spray of dirty plastic, corrugated cardboard, and metal lids.

"I hope it's a rescue," George muttered. He looked at the volcanoes around him, erupting gently with garbage, and then glanced at the sky. In the unchanging gloom he saw a bird that looked like a sheet of newspaper, folding and unfolding its wings.

A voice yelled in English and the truck began to roll away from him. George jumped up into the cab, kicking out at the scavenger nearest him. It occurred to him that he was having an adventure and that it was nothing like what he'd had in mind.

They arrived eventually at a structure that suggested a castle—an Erector set of discarded elements piled up in turrets and creakily crenellated supports. He was pleased to find that people did, indeed, speak English, though it was a kind of translator's English. It sounded like the directions you got from instruction sheets and manuals. A series of men wearing ruined hats said, "Please walk ahead slowly and to the right. Please handle calmly and pause." The speakers were as decrepit as the trash collectors on the hills, their clothes an odd assortment of rags, all run-down to the predominant gray color.

The doors in the castle were all perfectly good wooden doors, but they all had a fine powdery mold on them, and everything leaned or sagged against everything else. He pushed aside the door pointed out to him, then rubbed his palms against his shirt and checked to see if anything rubbed off. The room he entered was large and full of mended furniture settling into the floor at various angles.

"We welcome you completely," the attendant whispered and left.

George sighed. He was beginning to feel sleepy and hungry and rather conciliatory toward Laura. He was even beginning to worry about his job, and not his usual concern about whether it was too soon to call in sick, but whether he would ever see the dark, steady walls of the insurance company again.

He told himself bleakly that if you didn't like what you had, you got something worse. As if to prove his point, the filthiest person he'd seen yet came scuttling into the room, arms outspread expansively, his gray lips pulled back over yellowing teeth, murmuring, "Finally! Finally!" He grabbed George's shoulders and leaned down, twisting his face sideways into George's.

"A messenger from the Gods!" he crowed, spilling his stench into George's face. "Can you tell me what 'fresh-squeezed' means?" And with that he pinched George fiercely.

Laura, meanwhile, had definitely decided that her George went down the hole—just the kind of thoughtless, pointless, self-indulgent thing he'd do. She was furious. "Not in the least worried, not in the least," she kept saying with a quivering voice. "Just furious. These tears are the tears of rage."

She went to Roads, now the de facto authority on the hole, and demanded her husband back.

"I'm not suspicious by nature," Laura said. "At least I wasn't before I met George. So I don't know if he put you up to it or if it's some incredibly funny coincidence. Let me just say I'll forget the whole thing if you get him back here in time for supper." She crossed her arms on her chest and scowled with authority.

"Claims," Roads said smoothly, recognizing a no-win situation when he saw it. "You want Claims, not Roads. Small Claims down the hall and to the left, Large Claims one door past it."

Laura's fingers turned white as she continued to grip her own arms tightly. Roads smiled comfortingly. "Go to the second door," he said gently. "I can tell he's a large claim."

Laura unlocked her arms and turned out the door. "I want him back," she said stiffly.

"If he went down any of *my* roads we'll get him." He turned again to his report. It was wearing him down, these daily sessions ever since the hole had appeared. Everyone was caught up in the origins of the hole, the *meaning* of the hole. But unless someone actually figured it out—and soon—the only real, politic question was: What do we do with it now that we've got it?

The meetings were getting increasingly unruly, without a clear solution to the problem and without an official leader. The mayor was still consulting lawyers about the bribery charges, and no one expected anything of the deputy mayor.

"It's a good thing this isn't an election year," the deputy mayor said, "or we'd have to move a hell of a lot faster."

"This *is* an election year," Sewers pointed out.

"I'm an appointed official, so it's all the same to me," Traffic said. "But it's getting annoying. Either we close Main Street down permanently and divert to Elm, or we do something about that damn hole."

"Well, moving the traffic doesn't get rid of the hole, does it?"

"What if these things start popping up all over the place?" the deputy mayor asked with sudden interest.

"They don't pop *up* at all."

"Oh, technical talk. I'm impressed."

"Our real problem," Sanitation said, "is illegal dumping. My boys have seen people back down that street in the middle of the night and dump just about anything you could name down that hole."

When Roads heard this, his eyes turned bright and his brain went on overtime. He couldn't believe he was the only one in the room who understood that maybe the hole, wherever it came from and wherever it went, just might be the best thing to happen to Springer.

First thing in the morning, Roads was on the phone to the surrounding townships, jotting down notes and figures, consulting the county map. Within two days he was ready with his proposal at that day's meeting.

"That hole is the answer to everything," Roads said, with just the right amount of awe in his voice.

"That hole is nothing," Sewers said. "By definition."

"Joke of the day," the adjuster said dryly.

"You may not realize it," Roads continued, "but there's only one thing in this world that you can have too much of. And we're drowning in it." He looked impressively around the room. "Garbage."

"Where's this going?" Sanitation asked suspiciously.

"That hole takes everything. Everything. We can throw our garbage down it. Every town around can throw their garbage down it. We don't have to do a thing except collect the money." He leaned back expectantly.

"Well, I'm not at all against the revenue," Taxes said carefully. "But maybe there's more to it than meets the eye. This could back up on us somehow. I mean, how can we take advantage of something when we don't know the reason for it?"

"Reason!" Roads had a beatific flush on his face. "Who needs reasons as long as we have opportunities!"

"I can see this costing money," Budget said. "We'll need insurance—"

"It's not a through street anymore," Traffic objected. "You can't go all the way down Main Street now, you know, because of the hole."

"Yes, yes, we'll have to move things around," Roads said impatiently. "But I started calculating. I made some calls. We could get close to a million a month."

In the sudden silence that followed this figure most heads imagined what that money could do for their town, their department, their salaries. "That's a whole lot of money," Sewers said finally, and one by one everyone shifted slightly backward and smiled.

Before anything even became official, while the council members checked on impact for their individual areas, rumors spread through town, finally reaching the house where Laura, nerve-racked, still waited for her husband. The news catalyzed her. "They can't dump trash on George like that," she cried. Her mouth sagged, her eyes watered, and she finally made up her mind. Do or die, give or take, for better or for worse, she was going after George.

She slipped down the street at midnight, dressed in dark clothes, a scarf tied around her hair, thin-shouldered and sly, and she hesitated before she crossed each street, as if there were an enemy, an ambush, a law preventing her from finding George. The hole had been declared off-limits and she had never disobeyed anyone before.

She took deep, desperate breaths of air as she looked down at the hole and chose her moment, her heart thudding, her hands sweating. Then she put her hands over her face and stepped into the air.

The earth shifted under her and she swooped down, a breakneck slide that had no particular change in texture to it. When she finally came to rest, other things still moved past her and on her. She sat up, disoriented, her kerchief in one hand, an empty pill bottle in the other. The directions said, "Take one daily."

It was dim as she looked around. With every move she slipped a little further down in some kind of rubbish heap. Everywhere she looked, as far as she could see, was old garbage, giving off a sullen steam, occasionally rippling toward her or away from her. The thought that George must be somewhere cheered her up and gave her purpose. In a minute she chose a direction and took it. Having a purpose was reassuring, but what a strange place George had gotten to! And what was he doing here?

She knew, after all, that she had hit the largest garbage dump imaginable, that it stretched everywhere and seemed to be all there was. She could see figures on the hills and to the side sifting through the rubble or poking heads out suddenly to peer at her, their top lips curled back to reveal black teeth. She hissed at them.

She tried to keep track of landmarks as she walked—rusting, decayed heaps, silent slick pools. Certain objects coagulated together—egg cartons, old sofas, truck tires.

She came to the castle within an hour and she was searched by dirty hands connected to dirty men in dirty rags. She slapped at them and demanded George, taking refuge by barking out insults: "Brush your teeth! Take a bath! My God, you smell!" But that same idiotic curl to the upper lip was all that greeted her until one stepped forward and said, "This way to the center. Follow directions to the center."

The sagging halls they led her down were made of cardboard, magazines, paper plates, and napkins unidentifiably soiled. Her ardor was somewhat shaken; she was afraid that she, too, smelled bad by now, that it was past all possibility to be clean ever again.

She stood in a large room that seemed to be a waiting room, lost in thought, depressed by the filth, the stench, the apparent ceaselessness of filth. Where could it go? How would anyone ever get rid of it? Suddenly an arm snaked through an improvised doorway and an embarrassed face followed.

"George!" She took a step forward.

"Don't be too impetuous," he said, holding up a hand. "I've been here awhile, you know."

"And you never let me know! I've been sick with worry, sick with it!" She actually started to stamp her foot, but stopped when it made a sticking sound.

He rolled his eyes up. "Typical. Unreasonable. Irrational. Self-righteous. *Whine.*" He'd had time to expect her, to miss her, and to be angry at her for her absence. Only irritation had kept him focused while he waited for her; he was upset and he hated to be upset. Anger was safer. "I've found hundreds of phones, with no hookups. I found a mailbox, too, but as I'm sure *even you* can understand," he drew the words out as long as possible, "the mail collection's unreliable." He crossed his arms and glared at her triumphantly.

At this moment Laura noticed George's thin cheeks and his wrinkled, shredded clothes. It occurred to her how hard it must have been to survive here, and how noble he was to have done it. She had an impulse to ask him what he ate, but thought better of it. His thin cheeks made his eyes look luminous.

"Ah, George," she burst out, "it's been hell without you, hell!" "Hasn't it?" he asked after a stab of real anguish. His voice was softer and his shoulders relaxed. "Everything here rots. It just keeps coming through those holes, nothing clean, nothing healthy. And then I'd think of you and water and fresh air." He sighed. "You're here awhile and you begin to feel you deserve it." He shrugged his shoulders. "I think I recognize things, you know, in the garbage. I think I see a bike I had as a kid, or a chair we once had, or even a book I once read, and I go for it and I find it's junk, trash, sewage. Everything here reminds me of things I once loved."

Laura nodded. "For a moment I thought this was a castle."

"It is a castle," George said absently. "And I think about food and wrappings and packaging and chemicals. I think these pools, these puddles, are pesticides, drain cleaners, paint strippers, furniture cleaners. And how innocent they look in the stores! But everything ends up here! Do you know that?" He raised his eyebrows. "My garbage will live longer than *I* will. We've got to get out of here, Laura, because I don't understand who these people are and I don't know how they got here. I think they fell down a hole, just like me; and once they were just like me, but now there are moments…. I've got to get out of here, Laura, really I do. How did the world get to be like this? I'm beginning to expect it now; I'm beginning to fit in."

He looked at her with his luminous eyes, and Laura thought, faintly, that they were not the same color they had been, but she put the thought aside. "I came for you so we could go back together," she said simply.

"I thought maybe you would." He smiled. "I've looked around. I've seen the sea." He blinked at her unhappily. "It's not the same, it doesn't look the same. It's dark and the waves move slowly when they move at all, but it's big, and it's got to go somewhere."

"That's it, then," she said, suddenly gay. "We'll go to sea."

It took a day to reach the sea, and then another two days to build a raft. They ate whatever they could find that was edible, and even some things that were not, because nothing grew anywhere. There was plenty of discarded wood for their raft, and plastic ropes to lash wood together. They found stools and blankets and built a rude shelter, and they made a sail and two oars.

The ocean was ugly and heavy and stank of oil. At first Laura thought there were fish in it, but what she saw moving were clear plastic bags rushing up and down on the currents, or being dragged along on rusty cans and plastic bottles.

They pushed their raft out and used the oars to slice through the slick coat of oil and slide themselves forward over the sea. Once they were out of sight of land they were happier, and they began to talk of water as they once knew it, when it was clean and held life, when it smelled of salt and slapped in sprays. They were very careful not to touch it.

Springer's emergency town meeting had the best attendance record in memory. Roads was keenly aware of the excited surge of the crowd's murmur, of the glitter of eyes turning to him, watching his moves. The mayor had been arrested and everyone felt jubilant. A new election was only months away, and three people had slapped Roads on the back so far, throwing sentences at him that had the words "next mayor" in them. He felt exalted.

Everyone knew what the meeting was about, and Roads, as first speaker, went straight to the facts. He told them exactly how many townships he'd called so far, and how each and every single one had begged to send their garbage to Springer. Garbage was the problem of the decade, Roads said, and their town was in a position to be a problem solver, the most important town in the state, possibly in the nation. Sure, there were drawbacks—traffic for one, and garbage trucks in particular—but as he saw it, all that would happen would be that the town would become rich and no doubt spread upwind. Half the assembly grinned at that, and "upwind" made a little rippling dance across the rows. "There'd be no more taxes," he said finally. "Maybe even incentives, paybacks, shares for the inconvenience. It's possible." He shrugged and grinned. "That's just my opinion. I'd ask the mayor, you know, but he's got a different set of problems." He showed his teeth again, and the crowd went wild. He could hear the word "mayor" running down the rows like children, and it flushed him.

Sanitation spoke next and he was dour, complaining, and disliked. He didn't believe in magic, he said. He was sure that garbage went somewhere, but the audience shouted, "Prove it!" and he gritted his teeth and got nasty. They took a voice vote and everyone voted to make the hole into a landfill, which was the only legal way they could present it, and everyone on Main Street was to be compensated because their buildings had to be condemned. Owners of the condemned buildings slapped each other on the back and applauded Roads.

Everyone, in fact, was extremely happy. They chose two of the prettiest children in town and put them on a poster and pasted them all over the new routes into town.

They were the healthiest faces to be seen, with clean hair and clean white teeth and just the right amount of freckles. The children smiled with a clear blue sky behind them and flowers at their feet. The sign said: "Delightfully clean. Totally wholesome. Springer."

The Revolt of Everyday Things

Keys that jam, windows that won't budge. Fuses that blow when nobody's home. Jars that won't unscrew, doors that won't stay closed, milk that sours on its way home from the store. All these things were at war with Fran Rood—all these things and more. She didn't ordinarily complain so much (she didn't like people who complain so much), yet that was just another indication of how distinctly she felt at odds with the world. The things that were happening were the kinds of things that could happen to anyone, anytime; it's just that they were happening to her, and all at once.

"Well, so you've had a bad morning," her friend Becky said practically. "Maybe you should just call it quits and spend the rest of the day reading a book or watching the lake. That's bound to be safe."

"Who ever thought I would need a 'safe' day?"

" … while you consider what you're doing wrong."

"What in the world do you mean?" Fran felt her face freeze hard into a kind of dread. Did Becky see something obvious? *Should* this be happening to her? Or was this just the kind of statement a person who felt safe would make? Fran shook her head and laughed with determination. "You mean, not only is everything against me, but I deserve it, I provoke it, my pride has been found out?"

"I must be cheering you up; you're starting to sneer." Becky rose and stretched. "Walk me back and I'll find you a nice, comforting book.

You'll just have to take your chances with paper cuts." Becky headed around to the front of the house, following the rock path that Fran had laid in her garden. Fran's dog followed them jauntily, his tail held high, his mouth wide in a laugh. They all three walked down the small dirt road on the back side of the lake; it only took a few minutes before they turned down to Becky's house. Fran's eyes darted critically. As usual, Becky's lawn was cut to a nicety (the idea of what would happen if she touched a mower made Fran shudder), and she thought again how sad it was that Becky always chose geraniums in straight rows for her garden. It made Fran love her own garden more, if that was possible. In fact, one reason Becky and Fran remained friends was because each measured herself quite victoriously against the other.

When she got back, Fran sat down with the book in her hand. The back of the house faced the lake, and from her spot she could look straight across to where a clearing in the trees on the other side showed the main road ("main road" meant two lanes that were seldom used but, being a county road, was cleaned of snow in the winter). The only houses on the back road belonged to Fran and to Becky and her husband.

She sat down, facing the lake and the gap that displayed the road like a stage. An occasional car passed by, the dog went after a squirrel, and some birds chased each other across the skyline.

She continued to watch the lake and the gap in the trees with renewed confidence, until a red car crept slowly across the road on the other side of the lake. "Why, that's *my* car," she thought with surprise. It was the same make and model, certainly. It hesitated, as if staring at her. She had a common enough car, it was true. She thought nothing of it until the dog lifted his head, stood up, and ran off to the other side of the house. She got up to follow him.

She was surprised to see the red car pull in beside her own. The two sat there like twins, hers a little dustier and, to tell the truth, with the left parking light cracked from a bad decision on a recent jaunt to town.

A woman got out and walked toward her, stooping to fondle the dog, who behaved like an idiot. The dog had always been a cartoonish kind of dog, friendly and unfailingly happy. He was beside himself with joy now, squealing and wagging his tail, overdoing it as usual.

Fran came forward a few yards and then stopped, nonplussed. The woman getting out of the car looked like her-very much like her. Fran wore shorts that she had cut down from old jeans and an old shirt with paint stains on it. Her hair was pulled back with a clip, and she knew it wasn't flattering. She looked like herself on a bad day, and the woman now straightening up and advancing toward her with a yapping dog at her heels looked like Fran on a very good day indeed. Fran's hand went to her hair and then fell down; she was dismayed.

That cartoon of a dog circled the stranger in ecstasy, yipping madly. It was obviously the happiest day of his life.

"Hi," the woman said, holding out her hand. "I'm Ann Cross. I've come to see the house."

Her hair was recently cut. She wore carefully applied makeup. Her clothes were good and fit perfectly; they were understated and clever.

"The house," Fran repeated uneasily. She hesitated, feeling slow-witted as well as poorly dressed. She was at a disadvantage.

Ann Cross was looking around critically. "You have a lovely garden, really wonderful. I love delphiniums! I've always wanted to grow them but I've never had a garden before. I shouldn't say this, I know, but the garden is a selling point in itself." Her voice was friendly and warm and sounded eerily like Fran's voice on a tape recorder: both alien and familiar.

"Some people think hydrangeas are too old-fashioned," Ann continued, "but that's one of the things I like about them—that and the way they look." She laughed benignly; she had Fran's own laugh, only merrier. "In fact, this is the garden I always imagined, it's like a dream. Flax and foxglove and pinks. My grandmother had pinks, you know."

Fran murmured faintly, "I know," but Ann didn't hear her. "I bet that's heather, isn't it? That's exactly where I would put heather." She looked around her happily. "Peonies would do well here."

"The peonies bloomed last month. They're over there." Fran pointed. "Isn't it wonderful when everything finally falls in place?" Ann cried. "I never thought I would find a place like this-and so quickly! Such good luck! And the price is just in my range—well, actually, just a little bit above, but we can discuss that."

"Price of what?" Fran asked in what she hoped was a firm voice.

Ann stopped in her progress through the garden to peer at Fran with momentary puzzlement. "You *are* selling this house, aren't you?"

"No."

Ann covered her mouth with her hand quickly, a gesture Fran had used many times to cover embarrassment and confusion, as many women did. Ann very rapidly asked, "This is 13 Crescent Road, isn't it?"

"Yes." Fran saw herself as standing firm.

Ann reached into her pocketbook. "Could I use your phone and call the real estate agency? I'm horribly sorry, but they sent me here. Have they sent other people?"

"No. You're the only one." Fran was forced to lead the stranger into the house to use the phone. She stood nearby, her hands folded tensely as she listened to Ann's conversation. Ann hung up finally and turned to Fran with an apologetic smile. "This is so embarrassing. I made a mistake. I took the first left after the crossroad, not the first right. And it's 13 Pleasant Road, not 13 Crescent Road."

Fran looked disconcerted. "I didn't even know there was a lake over there. I've never bothered to go down that road."

"A pond, really."

"Well, this is a pond, too. We just call it a lake."

"And the house sounds exactly like this—a small ranch, just a half-acre. But no garden. It would take years to get a garden as good as yours. Are you sure you wouldn't sell?"

"But I love it here."

Ann sighed. "You're so lucky. This is just perfect. Two bedrooms? Do you have a porch?" She turned around. "Of course. The porch overlooks the lake. It's small but every part of it is perfect. I should go and see the other house. You've been very patient. I must have surprised you." She held up her hand. "But that's it. I'm on my way."

The dog wailed when she left; Fran had to hold him, struggling, in her arms. She went around the back of the house so that she could look across the lake, watching for the red car. It appeared and though Fran stood absolutely still, hoping she couldn't be seen, the car honked gaily and a hand appeared over the top, waving. Fran flinched.

She took the dog (who seemed annoyed with her) and rowed out on the lake, circling the edges carefully, her eyes always checking the road. When she got tired of that she went to her garden, pinching back flowers, turning the compost, digging up three plants and moving them an inch to the right, watering, staking. She was rough with her plants, as if they had to learn consequences.

It took almost two hours to quiet down again, convince herself it was a rank coincidence and not some further development in the war against her. Unfortunately, it was just at that point that the red car appeared again on the road across the lake.

Fran ran into the house and dialed rapidly. "Becky, this is an emergency. Get over here." She slammed the phone down and ran out the door, determined to stand guard at the end of her driveway.

The dog, thinking they were going for a walk, waited in the road, laughing and wagging his tail. When the car came toward them, his ears perked up and he began to bark a faith-restored bark, leaping at the car, his eyes squinting.

"I know I'm imposing," Ann said, slamming her car door with one hand and scratching the dog's ears with the other. "But I had to come back We have to talk"

Just then Becky came huffing down the road, her cheeks flushed and her eyes glittering. "What is it? What kind of call was that?" She was flushed with either excitement or anger and looked avidly at the stranger leaning against the car door.

"Hi," Ann said, sticking out her hand. "I'm Ann Cross. I'm here to convince this happy homeowner to sell her house."

Becky blinked. "I didn't know you were selling."

"I'm not."

"No, she really doesn't think she is," Ann said brightly. "But the fact is, I've fallen in love with her garden and her house and," bending down to be licked ecstatically, "even her dog. Are you a neighbor?"

Becky nodded.

"Well, I'm prepared to be a great neighbor to you, if you'll lend me your support." She turned to Fran. "I saw the other place; it's like this place only without a soul. Or a heart. Or whatever. I pulled in and yawned. I nearly fell asleep on my feet, walking around it. It may be under some form of enchantment, waiting for the evil to be undone. But I know that I had to come back here. This really does suit me, you know. I'd be a fool to just shrug and drive away." She smiled most appealingly. "I don't even know your name, so I couldn't call you. I just want you to think about selling this house. I'd pay you a better price than you could get from anyone else. Just think about it, that's all I ask You may find it's time to move on anyway." She smiled and turned, linking her arm in Becky's, and said, "You really have to help me, you know, if we're going to be neighbors. I look on you as an ally. We'll be great friends, you'll see.

I make a great friend." Her voice had a subtle enticing lilt to it. She was entirely believable.

Becky seemed happy to be taken up so quickly. She adapted Ann's easy, chummy style. "But what can I do?" she cried.

"Just help me. Support me. I don't ask much, I never have. All I've ever wanted is a garden like this, just this one thing." Ann was innocent and gay. "It's all I really want," she confided. "Can't she want something else?" "Oh, that's very funny," Becky said, amused. "You should get what you want, of course you should."

"That means I would lose what I want," Fran protested.

"Well then, maybe you could take turns?" She grinned at Fran and winked at Ann.

"I don't know why you're talking this way, agreeing with her. This is mine; I've worked hard. Why should someone else take it?"

"You see how it is," Ann sighed. "It always comes down to possession, not right."

"But it *is* right. It's right for me to have what I worked for."

"Oh, I could work for it too, you know. Anyone who did that work would have that garden. Maybe I would work harder and have an even better garden. If all you think about is work" She smiled again and stooped to pet the dog. "But I'm annoying you by being so honest, and that's just hurting my case. I'll call you again sometime when you're calmer. I'll talk to you then."

She slipped back into her car, ignoring the dog's grief, and drove off. The two women stared at her retreating bumper. Becky finally turned to Fran. Becky looked suddenly a little drawn, the way one looks when a drink has worn off. "That was it? You just wanted to show me your buyer?"

"Her name is Ann Cross. Mine is Fran Rood."

"So?"

"You know that a rood is a cross?"

"No, I didn't know."

"She looks like me."

Becky cleared her throat tentatively.

"We could be twins."

"Well," Becky said gently, "you know, she's a bit thinner than you are."

Fran blinked at her and cocked her head. "She even sounds like me."

"In a vague kind of way, I guess. I hadn't noticed."

"She wants my home."

"She wants your *house*," Becky corrected, and sighed. "You're having a bad day, you told me so yourself. Take it easy. I didn't see what you saw, I didn't hear what you heard. Maybe you should think about this without so much prejudice." She nodded to herself, satisfied.

"She said she came here by accident, drove right up to my door," Fran said stiffly. "You don't see anything odd in all this?"

"Oh, odd," Becky shrugged. "Odd things happen all the time. In fact, odd things are normal. Don't worry; it's over." She was already heading off down the road, her voice trailing listlessly off.

Normal or not, Fran couldn't accept the oddness of it all. When she was very small, there was a girl in her class with the same first name, and she was a very stupid little girl, unsure of her answers and apt to cry. Fran became an aggressive know-it-all because she was certain that everyone would confuse her with the other girl. Even though Fran always got gold stars on all her tests, she felt that the other girl was marring her somehow, that she couldn't avoid being compromised because of the correspondence between them.

It was like that now, only worse, because it was obvious that this double of hers, Ann Cross, was stronger than she was. She had managed to convince Becky, for instance, that there was no resemblance at all when Becky should have sided with Fran. And she'd enraptured the dog.

Fran by now was sitting at the back of the house, watching the road across the lake. She was on guard. Her gaze was so intense that she was pretty well mesmerized, and her heart started skipping with an awful thud when a part of the ground near a tree rose and started moving away.

It was absurd of course, merely the dog moving, merely some kind of trick of the eye or trick of the mind. Fran shook herself to get rid of the feeling—an awful, suspicious feeling that the campaign against her had stepped up a notch. She could be fooled; she was liable to surprise attacks.

Ann Cross, however, did not return that day or the next. On the third night Fran woke up in the darkness as the dog whined beneath her bed. She was suddenly awake and alert, but with no reason for it. Had she heard something? Was it thunder? Was it wind? Lying in bed, she turned to the window where a dim glow from the moon cast dark mounds of shadows on the pane. One shadow looked like a head.

Quietly, noiselessly, Fran raised herself up to peer out the window. A cloud moved away from the moon, causing a sudden shift in the pattern of light, and she saw a face staring in at her, a face unmistakably surprised, its mouth rounded at being caught.

Fran leaped from her bed and grabbed a bat that she kept by the door. The dog yelped in excitement and glee, and Fran turned on the outside lights and ran out, hatred, anger, livid revenge roaring in her heart. There was no doubt in her mind that it was Ann's face she had seen, not her own reflection on the glass.

The dog ran to all the corners of the light, wagging and barking. He distrusted darkness and steered clear of it. If this was a game, he loved it and flung himself around, daring himself to touch the very edges of darkness itself, toying with it.

Fran heard something crashing off through the trees. She was shocked that Ann had gotten here, in the night, without her car, but she was utterly convinced that it was so. This merely indicated some renewed resolution on Ann's part.

Well, she had renewed resolution of her own. In the morning she drove her red car over to the other house on the other lake, the one that was for sale.

It was eerily similar to hers, on a road behind a lake, but the land did not slope as much and the road was paved. As Ann had said, there was no garden, just a lawn and a lot of gay red and yellow lawn ornaments. It could have been lifted up in one strip and put down anywhere, anywhere at all, without suffering incongruity.

It was owned by a couple moving to Florida; they were cheerful and practical, pointing out improvements they had made that Fran had never gotten to. But Fran kept looking through the windows to the lawn and "the views," as the owner kept saying, "the views which are so pretty, every season." There was a lake outside their window, just as there was one outside hers. The window was even the same size.

Fran drove furiously home. As she passed a gap in the trees, she looked across the lake to her house and saw a woman sitting in her chair, with her dog at her feet, by her house. She gripped the steering wheel to keep from driving straight across the water. Was the world shifting, and should she have been smarter and stayed home? Was reality basically a question of location, placement? Fran's head buzzed and she shivered, and it occurred to her that it would be ironic if Ann actually lived there with "her" dog and this was all a delusion on Fran's part. After all, Fran thought, grinding her teeth, she had just come back from viewing a house for sale. Perhaps she was insane. Briefly, the idea gave her comfort. Insanity was at least a way out.

But she couldn't kick the idea, when she drove up, that it was *her* house and *her* dog and that insanity was a stale excuse.

Ann sauntered up to her, grinning, the dog at her heels. Her red car was sitting where Fran's was normally parked and the cars' bumpers looked like mocking smiles.

"I had to see it again, to make sure it was every bit as good as I remembered."

Fran swept past her to the chair in the back of the house, which she picked up and moved three inches. She sat down and crossed her arms, staring with a stiff jaw at the lake. "You're trespassing."

"Oh. I'm sorry. I didn't think you'd mind. I'm just visiting." She smiled shyly, prettily, winningly. Fran, with a shock, realized that she must be capable of that smile herself, or some version of it. "I thought, you know, that we could talk. A garden like that shows your personality. I like your garden. I must like you. I thought we could be friends."

Did Fran's own voice have that undercurrent of sincerity, of warmth? Probably some version of it, Fran thought with despair, some version with less likability, too much sincerity, heat instead of warmth. What made Ann dangerous was how convincing she was.

"No," she said, and kept her eyes away from Ann's face so that she wouldn't see how she reacted. Whatever Ann's response—disappointment, resolution, contempt—it would be the perfect embodiment of that emotion on that kind of face. Just as Ann looked like Fran, only better, so all her actions, words, and gestures were like Fran's—only better. Perhaps, Fran thought uneasily, hoping that Ann would leave if she was ignored, perhaps she is actually the expression of my intentions.

"Well," Ann finally said, her voice tinged with a delicate apology, "I shouldn't have come unannounced. I have your number now; I'll call first next time."

"Please don't. There's no reason to come back."

Ann paused and then said with firm politeness, "There's always a reason, if it's what you want. And I like your garden. I said that." There was no hint of animosity or satisfaction. She stood behind Fran quietly; a sense of inevitability radiated from her.

For all Fran knew, Ann could come and stand in the road and look at her garden, polite and friendly to the neighbors, an appealing victim should Fran try to turn to the law. She could already see Ann's open and pleasing smile: "It's the garden that brings me here. I dream about her garden. I'm at the edge of paradise, just peeking in." How could Fran triumph over such innocence, such grace? All of Fran's attempts to assert her ownership, her privacy, would merely be the posturings of greed and arrogance; she could see her failed attempts at her feet already, like a November garden. She sat, her chin resting on her chest. Her eyes looked out around her, and it seemed unreasonable to be expected to give it up. She was used to this scene, the sound of the bird now calling in the trees, and even though it might be time to give someone else a chance at it—the concept of privilege had always worried her—she saw no reason to give it up to Ann, who already got the world to do her bidding.

She rose up, standing straight as a tree, and then turned to face Ann. She hoped her smile was wide and convincing. "I don't think I've been sympathetic enough; I don't think I've understood how pure your wishes are. I admire wishes, I really do, I've had a few of them myself." She nodded and pointed the way to the garden, excusing herself for a moment. "I'll be right back, right back, smell the viburnum, it's late this year"—and when she returned she carried a large watering can. She began to pour its contents (thicker than water normally was) over the viburnum and the hydrangea, careful not to spill anything on the lawn. She dripped the liquid over the leaves and around the branches, making her way down the row of bushes. Her smile was stretched thin.

Ann sniffed and her nose screwed up into a knot of concern that spread outward on her face. "What is that?" she asked. "What are you doing?"

Fran put down the can and reached into her pocket for matches. A breeze blew the first one out, but she cupped the second match successfully and bent over like a vestal. The bush lit up quickly in an almost phosphorescent flash, releasing a sweet and acrid smell. The heat ballooned out, the bush wavered, and then the bush next to it went poof! and down the row the leaves twisted and the branches reached up—hydrangea, mock orange, buddleia—spitting and puffing.

The heat waved out toward them, bending the long flowers on their stems, their heavy heads cringing to the ground. Fran bent over also and began to grab the flowers, pulling them roughly out of the ground or simply snapping them in half, tossing them into the flames.

"What are you doing?" Ann cried, her voice outraged.

Perhaps she hadn't used enough lighter fluid; the fire began to die down quickly. Fran continued to pull out plants. "Help me, why don't you? We have to make sure nothing else catches." The bushes, shrunken and nude, smoked and shook in front of them.

Becky rushed down the driveway, her arms waving. "What happened? What happened? What's all this smoke?" For a second all three of them paused and looked around, as if out of politeness.

Becky broke the spell. "Where's your hose?" she cried and, as Fran pointed, she turned on the tap and aimed it at the bushes, producing a pale, exhausted steam as Fran continued to pull out plants.

"You can stop that now," Ann said sullenly.

"It feels too good to stop," Fran answered, her eyes like stones. But she did stop, and turned to survey her garden. What hadn't been destroyed had been trampled. Of course the damage was confined to one section, but it was the best section, she thought with satisfaction. How odd that destroying it would involve such pleasure, such a sense of regained control. "Looks ruined to me," she said cheerfully to Ann. "What do you think?"

Becky leaped around from edge to edge, drenching everything. "Surely you realize you've gone too far?" Ann asked in a cold voice. "Oh, I didn't mean to do it," Fran said breezily. "I just wanted to burn some leaves and it got out of control. I've been messing up lately." "It's true," Becky called. "Everything's been going wrong with her."

"Why did you do that?" Ann's voice was pitched low; she leaned toward Fran so that Becky couldn't hear.

Fran smiled again. She thought it must be a wonderful smile, perhaps as good as Ann's smile, perhaps better. "Well, it was my garden after all. The nice thing about having anything is that you can change it, no matter who's watching, no matter what they think." She beamed at Ann. "You'll never get this garden, you see."

"Is that why you did this? You're insane. How could I take it from you? I could never force you to give it to me."

"You can't now," Fran said reasonably. "And I know it. It's nothing you want now." She looked around with fresh eyes. "Maybe I'll put in a plain lawn," she thought. "Or a vegetable garden. Maybe I'll grow corn." She nodded. "Or pave it. The future is open."

Becky attacked a pile of smoldering leaves with vigor. She got a stick and pushed the leaves apart, layer by layer, drenching it all.

"You're crazy, you know," Ann said politely. "I could never have taken it away from you." She turned to go. Maybe she was nervous or rattled by the afternoon's events, but she stepped into Fran's car by mistake. She tried her key over and over again, scowling. Fran felt beatific. She laughed and spread her arms wide, walking toward Ann, whose scowl changed to a look of dread as she approached.

"Oh what a day!" Fran shouted. "And you're in the wrong car!"

Ann slammed the door hard as she moved to the other car. "You look like a maniac," she cried spitefully, but she was bested and Fran could see it. Nonchalantly, Fran picked up a stone and, as Ann started her car, threw it at the front left light, smashing it. The two cars now looked identical.

Fran serenely waved good-bye. Her dog whined only slightly at her ankles. She turned toward the house; there wasn't all that much to do if gardening was abandoned. She looked critically at the waste around her. Becky threw the hose down and shut the water off. "Honestly, Fran," she said, "it must be something in your attitude, it really must. I've never run across anyone with the kind of luck you have."

"Yes," Fran said absently, "but I really do feel it's turned."

"I guess it would have to." Becky brushed herself off and started for home. Fran followed companionably.

"I'm going to miss that garden of yours," Becky said. "I liked looking at it, and on humid nights the scent of it came all the way over here."

"You could grow the same things."

"Geraniums are the only things I can keep alive."

"I could help. It's the least I can do for a friend. We'll get you some sweet smelling roses tomorrow, some old-fashioned ones. You'll see. Roses got me started."

Becky was interested. "If you think I could actually do it ... well, I'd be grateful forever."

"Of course you can do it," Fran insisted. "In a year or two you'll have the best rose garden in the county."

"I've always wanted a real garden." Becky smiled and nodded and went into her house. Fran waved and turned back down the road. The dog barked once and trotted behind her.

Overpowering Joy

For all of her married life, Tillie Sullivan had looked at the lake and gathered peace from it. She'd been able to accommodate loss when her husband died, had bent to it. When grief threatened to twist her with its weight, she had always walked down to the earthen dam, to look over the water to the rising hills, the standing trees, and back to her home.

When the dam started to give way in a violent storm and the authorities stepped in and condemned it, Tillie had adjusted her shoulders and prepared for more weight.

They opened the valve to the spillway and the lake drained away, week by week, and most of the fish made their way through the spillway and down a stream to the next lake below. Now when Tillie stood on the dam and looked at the lake, all that was left was a huge puddle, not more than eight inches deep. Day by day the puddle turned sluggish, the rippling of its fish attracting the sturdy, dedicated watching of the blue herons, the dead fish rising up sporadically, mouths open, discarded. The lake bed lay naked and unfleshed.

When she looked to the other side of the dam, the spillway trickled into two pools that fed the stream. In the recesses of the pools, small flits of movement scuttled away, fish trapped by an unmannerly tide. They had just room enough to shuttle, with little opportunity for true hiding.

Tillie Sullivan saw the fish dart and climbed down for a closer view. The growth behind the dam was skewed trees, mountain laurel, fiddlehead fern, and huge clusters of skunk cabbage. The lushness and damp of the runoff stream generated a crowd of flies and gnats, mosquitoes and bees, that swung around the old woman in Brownian motion. She shook her head and surveyed the landscape as the pool narrowed into the stream. Tillie turned and followed the stream, her eye measuring each dip and twist. The stream would normally have been dry this time of year, long past the spring thaws and runoffs that usually raised the lake's level. But now it had settled down to a few deep pockets and then a damp, rocky water bed for perhaps a quarter of a mile before it ran into the next lake. Tillie tried to look at it all from what she would have termed a fish's perspective. The stream ran downhill; when filled with the lake's runoff, it had been a rushing rill, fraught with rapids and waterfalls and logjams of fallen branches and saplings.

Tillie took in the route and climbed back to the overflow pipe. She was not overtired, though at her age she always expected to be, no matter how minimal the effort.

She stood, again, at the first pool, straightening her back and dusting the twigs and gnats from her hair. To her left a dead fish floated. She broke a length from a fallen birch and prodded the fish out of the water. Spotted newts scattered at her movements; flies made furious dives at the fish.

"Whatever's left is just left to die," she said out loud. She had started talking out loud about a year after her husband died. For a while she had talked to Martin, but then that had passed and now she just made comments to keep her voice in tune.

She climbed back up the dam, grabbing at brush and exposed roots on the way. Once there, she straightened again, and again dusted her hair. From this view, what was left of the lake was right below her, still rippling with life. Every morning now she came upon the herons-slow-motion strollers-as they fed upon the fish. She watched them as they took off at her approach, the staggering effort it took for those wings to lift. She always marveled at how she could see each wing beat; she could even see their bellies as they spiraled up and over her.

"Breathe in, push harder," she called out to them, her head craned up to their slow rise.

The herons weren't there now. But at the perimeters of the puddle were more dead fish. She scrambled slowly down the inside rim of the dam, pulling a stick behind her to pry the fish out of the water. There was a scum forming along the edges.

Ever since the dam had started to give way, she had watched the water recede as the lake emptied out. She had faith that there would be a lake again; even if she had to rebuild that dam by hand. For over forty years she and Martin had gotten out of bed to take a first look at the lake. She had swum in it, skated on it, seen beaver and muskrat and every kind of duck stroke their way across it. She had watered her lower garden from it, had planted a weeping willow to drift into it and ladled out the silt from her area so the weeds wouldn't grow.

The lake was as much a part of her as the flowering quince and the blueberry and raspberry bushes she'd planted and that were now as thick as walls. This landscape was her life, as intimate to her as the seasons themselves—marked by thaw, flood, heave, and freeze.

"Once this was mine," she said, back at her house and gazing steadily down from her porch to the drained, nude bottom of the lake. Her porch was patched with old screen work, sewed and salvaged over the years. Here she kept birdseed, rake, shovel and hoe, pickax and rocker. From the center she sorted the landscape around her. The feeders hung from trees and hid in bushes, calling goldfinch and purple finch, nuthatch and siskin, cowbird and hummingbird, grosbeak and cardinal. Each bird marked a particular season—nuthatch and holly, robin and crocus, house finch and lilac, oriole and azalea. All of these were carefully tuned; she would note the arrival of the phoebe and pinch off a hyacinth.

The punctuality of the details kept her alive. Every season she repaired, constructed, reinforced; she turned the compost, gathered the kindling, divided the irises, cleared the gutters. In winter she crocheted to keep her hands moving, hauled deer feed and salt licks to keep her back strong, made birdhouses to keep her spirits high.

Years ago, whenever Martin caught fish for supper, she had tossed bread into the water to balance it out.

Her hair was white and cut close to her head. Her face reflected its progress through the seasons, tanned and lined from the months she spent outdoors—pruning, hacking, cutting, lifting. She had learned to chop wood after her husband died, had moved into his plaid shirts and overalls, adapted his hats, assimilating him after his death so that in many ways she looked like him, having even adopted his slow, deliberate walk. "Martin never wasted a motion," she said, remembering him. Whether Martin would have approved of her plan now, have helped her or shook his head in slow disbelief, she couldn't tell. Martin had merged, after his death, into a kind of alter ego; he was now simply a state in her life, like her youth. When she looked at her hands they reminded her of Martin's hands: gnarled, sturdy, the nails broken only by work.

She was not about to let those fish die. She told herself it was not sentimentality, but a rigid naturalism. Accidents were part of the environment, but accidents should be swift and never encouraged. Too much was arbitrary; too much was lost.

She brought out two spades and the pickax and hunted out her heavy work gloves. She headed back down the road to the dam. It was still early morning; she could get a lot done. The stream's path was treacherous and uneven; she would have to clear that. The pool where the fish were now hiding should be widened, if possible. The puddle that was the lake was lower than the opening to the spillway. Right now a heap of rocks slowed down the spill out of the lake. She would have to reinforce the rocks to keep more water from draining, then dig a trench back to the puddle so that when the makeshift sluice was opened, the fish could move freely.

This was all aimed to hold the fish until a good rain came, at which time she could remove her blockages and let the water and the fish spill down the stream to the next lake.

"Logical place to start is the spillway," she said, straightening up as she stood on top of the dam. Below her spread the lakebed, cracked silt along the outer edges, mud and trickles running together in the center. She took one spade with her and shifted her way down the dam.

"Worst part's the mud," she muttered. She always wore boots until high summer, so the only problem with the mud was the difficulty in moving. She gathered dead leaves, twigs, and stones from the ground and wedged them into the rocks already forming a minidam for the sluice.

She kept at it, adding more rocks until there was only the merest trickle. Then she began her trench, keeping her back as straight as possible. The water made it easy to dig and move the silt, but it was so fine that half of it clouded back into the trench. She reduced her efforts, moving only small sections, not lifting them out of the water but shifting them up the wall of the trench as she created it. Smaller efforts and controlled movements minimized the sweep back of the silt. She worked steadily and slowly, straightening up every few minutes to prevent the stiffness in her back from getting serious. "Can beat any pain, any pain, if you work with it. Only a fool works against it, or lets it work against her," she said.

The digging made her think of other diggings. She and Martin had cleared the scrub around their house, long ago, and put in a lawn. She had dug out the holes for all her bushes, had dug out and moved the many rocks that had countered her gardening plan. One rock had almost defeated her: she'd exposed it and could only get it out by prying it slowly, inches at a time, and pushing smaller rocks under it to raise it up. That one she had asked Martin to move to the center of the lawn, where she liked to consider it an award, one surrounded by successive blooms of crocus, tulip, and daylily.

She worked at the trench until she wearied of her motions, "Boredom being the worst thing," then left her spade and climbed down the other side. Already she preferred this side for working on, though the heavy growth slapped branches at her arms and the mosquitoes and gnats hit her face like spit. The shade and the very denseness made the place wilder, secretive. Tillie took care of the dead fish first, since the stench spread around her like a physical swarm. She dug a hole and buried the ones she'd moved earlier, covering them quickly. The size of some of the fish surprised her. Somehow she had never been interested in learning their names. Martin had fished and cleaned his catch; she'd merely eaten whatever he'd taken, having no fondness for them. But as she gathered the corpses she took note of their distinct shapes and colorings. "I would call this one a large-mouth bass," she said, picking it up on her shovel and moving it to its grave. It was all of a foot long, speckled or mottled, and with a blunt curved head like a dolphin. Its mouth was huge, "from ear to ear," and she noted with interest that it seemed to have teeth. Having buried it she knelt down beside the pool, looking carefully for the other fish.

There were sunnies, round and quick, which she knew because sunnies kept to the shallower waters down by her dock, swishing their fins in one set spot so the ground beneath them was cleared in a circle.

There were long tiger-striped fish. "Would that be a pickerel? A long, striped name." And fatter, white-bellied fish. "Perch? To rhyme with birch? Both white-barked?" She leaned closer over the pool, her face only inches now from the surface. The newts drifted and flicked in the shallows. Tillie began to move rocks as she peered intently. "Which ones are you?" she whispered. "Who gave you names and why are you hiding from me?" She took off a glove and lowered her hand open-fingered into the pool. "Come, this one, that one, no harm in me." And her hand swept gently through the pool, stirring up the silt, causing her to lose sight of fin and tail.

At once it flashed into her head what it would be like to live in that pool. Dark, silent, and, when they made it to freedom, clear.

Her back hurt at staying bent over for so long. She stood up, twisting from side to side to loosen it. Then she took up her spade and worked at the pool. It was easier work; there was more gravel and sand than silt, and it was possible to heft neat packages out of the water and onto the land. The rocks moved easily once she cleared around them. A fish came flipping through the spillway and landed flat on the gravel. She grabbed it and laid it in the pond, where it came to life. She dug out the earth around the pipe until it made a safe channel and went back to the pool. She laid aside the shovel and dug out the rocks and stones with her bare hands. The water became even murkier, but she could see that the pool was growing nicely. She scrabbled and dug and pushed, "Making butter, baking bread."

She widened the first pool and cleared the pathway to the second. She pulled out two fallen hickory logs, tugging and grunting. A pair of chipmunks reared back and chittered at her. Once again she plunged her hands in to scoop up rocks and to tug at buried branches. She worked until the nails on her fingers bent back. She watched as a fish flopped sideways through her channel from the first pool to the second.

She continued her chore, day after day, for over a week Each day she dipped her hand into the pool and it swam after the fish. Each day she buried the dead and cleared more growth out of the stream. She began to watch the sky for clouds. "No thunder, no lightning, just a big bucket turning over," she warned, and kept her wading boots by the porch door.

The day that the rain came Tillie was almost unable to get out of bed, her back was so stiff and sore. She allowed herself to moan as she reached over to the bedpost and pulled herself up. "Dignity, dignity," she spat out. "Someone else's word."

She dressed in her overalls, made a cup of tea, and sat out on the porch. The sky was thick and dark and the air was so heavy it weighed everything down. The arm of the rocker was damp to the touch.

The rain didn't start until afternoon. Tillie waited it out, drinking cups of tea and rocking. All her chores were done—the feeders were stocked with seed, the windows were shut against the rain, the house was swept clean. She rocked slowly as the clouds massed, gathering strength, filling with resolve.

The first drops came as a rush of noise from the other side of the lake, running toward her. Tillie waited to see that it was a good, solid downpour, not some bankrupt shower. She watched as the water poured down the gutters and spilled into cracks on the ground, making quick small springs. There was no sound of bird or beast above the rain, and even the edges of the trees were blurred in the general hurry.

The path to the dam was already turning into a mud slog. Tillie was satisfied to see the runoff making tracks to the lakebed. She imagined the water filling the lake again, the fish greedily lapping at it.

At the dam she surveyed the lakebed, observing the flash streams flowing in, her wet hair capped tightly against her head, the clouds promising more. She slid down to the spillway, pawing aside the rocks and branches she'd piled up against the sluice, and watched the water flow. She took her spade and made sure that her trench still held, and she stepped through the water calling, "Move out, move out! Last chance!"

She climbed over to the other side. Water was rushing out of the drainpipe with a rich sound. She plunged past the pools to see if the stream was filling, if it was strong enough to carry the fish down below. Everything held. "A river," she said. "I've created a river," and it was a satisfying sight indeed as the water rushed higher than she'd even hoped, churning and pushing.

She went back to the drainpipe. Already fish were coming through—difficult to see amid the tumult except for a sudden glitter or flash.

Tillie laughed once happily as she saw with satisfaction how well it worked. She freed more rocks and branches to speed the water along: the stream itself ripped the rocks from her hands, pulling them along like boats.

The rain poured down, poured down. The water ran into every runnel and rut, sweeping swiftly down to the lakebed, from the lakebed to the pools, from the pools to the stream. The branches bent with the weight of the water, the grasses lay low and swept it on. Tillie held her hand out to collect more of it, turned her hand over and gave it to the stream.

She went back to the first pool, the pool that had so strangely caught her eye. There was a torrent now streaking from the drainpipe, bubbles were appearing on the surface of the water. It was difficult to distinguish anything. Where were her fish? Where were the beloved fish? She knelt down, her knees sucked into the mud. She took off her gloves and rolled up her sleeves, plunging her arms in up to the elbows, feeling her hands begin a life of their own, looking for fish. She could feel nothing, and plunged her face into the water, lowering her head to see. Below the surface, the fish were in a tumult. Tillie could see them come racing in from the drainpipe, hurled in a curve and then straightening out. They brushed against her face, what must have been to them a strange stone. They scurried off into groups huddling around the underground roots, dashing under a submerged leaf. Their grace was overpowering and Tillie moved her lips to say something encouraging and loving to them. Her hair must have appeared to some fish like weeds, for the smaller ones made darts at her, which was not displeasing.

The fish continued to tumble, until the pool seemed to writhe with them. Tillie got up again and began to move aside the stones and leaves of her minidam. It was time for the fish themselves to be swept through, downstream, into the next lake. Her heart no longer wanted to do it, however; she wanted to keep the fish, keep them in this small pool. Sense told her they would not be able to survive there for long, that very soon she'd be burying them as they strangled, too confined.

She removed the last of the large rocks, and the water rushed through with the flitter and thump of the fish it contained. The speed and force widened the passage she'd made, making a smoother transition. Tillie knew that her plan had worked, that the fish would be gone with the water, with the puddle, with the pool. She returned to kneel by the pool and sank her head into it. There was a small whirlpool there now, as the water came through the drainpipe, swirled around, and headed out into the stream. She raised her head and gasped for air, lowering it again. She put her shoulders under as well, and her hands went out for the fish, grasping them and directing them through to the stream. Her mouth worked; she cheered them on. She rose, choking and sputtering, and then went in again, working with the rain to move every movable object on earth. And when she was through, she thought she could not bear the utter emptiness of it and dived into the pool, her hands seeking more fish. Her mouth called out to them to wait for her, her eyes open and unblinking, but she was far too large for the pool or the stream and the running water pushed her out again at the very channel she'd dug to the stream. She lay there gasping and shivering, thinking of herself as scaled and drowning before she remembered who she was. That night she slept with mud still on her hands. She dreamed of swimming with the others down an endless fluid path. And when she spoke, strange mouths answered.

Ghost Nets

Rachel rowed sometimes, and then her father rowed. He was a square man, taut-skinned and solid. He had a gray mustache and short gray hair, which he brushed with his hand when he was tired instead of rubbing his eyes. His eyes were brown.

Rachel always called him Papa. It was a name that caused him to pause, split second, when she said it. He would have felt more comfortable with his own name, Wendell Dupeen, or Wen, as his friends called him. He had no objection to having a daughter; he rather enjoyed it, in his own taciturn, slow-turning way, but he had never gotten used to "Papa."

Rachel was fifteen. She still went out with him, fishing late at night for pleasure or early morning for work. In a year or two, he supposed, this would stop.

She wore her hair braided in two plaits down her back, shrugging them over her shoulder when they wandered forward, even tying them in a knot when they threatened to get in the way. He approved of her: long legged, skinny, sunburnt nose, loose shop-print dresses she'd outgrown (shapeless things, really, but on Rachel you saw they were a covering, not an advertisement).

Rachel was quiet when she was around her father. After all, he was a silent man. She had learned to read his eyes and the lines around his cheeks to know what he was thinking, and those lines, on a brilliant moonlit night out in the channel, with the slap of the water and the slap of the oars, were conversation enough. Rachel could handle silence; she wasn't yet made uneasy by it.

Nighttime fishing was the best because it didn't matter if you caught anything. No need to check the charts, the calendar, or the logbook Wen kept on the fish. It was done for yourself, for the simple, silent, bracing, awful beauty of the sea. Things could be laid to rest at night, little things that otherwise smoldered or nicked at your skin. When everything was out of sight but the dim edge of the horizon, when there was no voice but the hum of the sea, what did anything matter? Rachel could understand her father's silences; they washed him clean.

So that night—full moon hung almost orange, blotting out the stars—both kept a companionable quiet. Everything had already been said anyway. Fishing was bad; that is, the trade was bad. Fish rolled up by themselves on the shore, belly-up, bloated. "Red tide," the knowing ones said. Meanwhile, rowboats, motorboats, small trawlers smacked hungrily in the bay, tied up and leaking oil.

The bay itself looked like a picture of Greece that Papa had once shown Rachel. Water, then houses along the shore, then steep hills hanging over the water jutting with more houses. But Greece was warm and very likely didn't have the red tide, or the bacteria that crept in and killed the oyster beds, or the mysterious iodine level that kept the lobsters off the market.

Fishermen were never rowdy, as far as Rachel knew. From her experience they were a band of tight-lipped men and women who looked out to sea quickly, briefly, as if avoiding a disappointment, who studied the notices tacked on the pier with pretended indifference, if not scorn.

The great tuna days were over: the large fleets had taken off, hauling them in like rice. Bluefish, flounder, any fish paid little and sometimes showed in such poor numbers that it would have been cheaper to leave the boat home.

More and more people were turning away from the sea. The richer ones, those capable of judging events as a trend rather than a circumstance, had started looking elsewhere years ago. They sold what they had and moved inland or, like the ex-mayor, turned their houses into hotels, bed-and breakfast places with checkered curtains and racks of picture postcards, all of them over twenty years old, showing men hauling in their catch. These men, twenty years later, looking more than twenty years older, would stop by the little shop for cigarettes or matches and hold the cards in their callused, scarred hands, for a moment rueful and indulgent. Imagine! They thought it would last forever! The first shipment of cards had been sold to the men themselves, or to their wives and sweethearts, and cards all over the island lay hidden in drawers or packed in the bottom of a souvenir box up in the attic. They were even used as memorials, sometimes, when relatives visited old or new graves: a picture postcard, the color a little too alert, maybe even slightly out of register, propped against a headstone, or held down by a rock so the wind wouldn't blow it away.

There was always a wind, even when there were no fish. Rachel liked to stand at the end of the bay where it jutted out to sea, leaning against the seawall, the fantastic wind holding her pigtails straight out behind her, whipping her dress around her thighs, her eyes squinted into the air, wet just from the water the wind carried.

Her father lit a cigarette. On dark nights she would watch the burning ember so she could locate where his face was. On a bright night such as this she watched the smoke spread around him and disappear like a fog. He looked around him carefully, as if there were variations on the surface of the water that would tell him where the fish he sought were hiding. She believed it was possible. She had read that robins could see the vibrations of an earthworm tunneling underground. If so, why not her father catching vibrations of the fish?

When he was done with his cigarette, he threw it on the water and they both watched the small white speck bobbing on the waves. In a minute an unseen mouth took it. Rachel imagined its dumb disappointment: the acrid, brown taste.

Her father jerked slowly on one oar, moving them farther out. He had made up his mind about where they'd fish.

Rachel dipped into the bucket of bait and slipped a herring onto her hook She trailed her line slowly from the back of the boat, as her father maneuvered into place. She carefully buttoned her thick wool sweater. Wen never seemed to notice the cold and disliked it when she shivered—it meant he would have to take her back. He often gave her his own sweater, when he wore one, but once Rachel got cold it seemed she couldn't get warm, and he could tell by the way she huddled (knees drawn together, arms around them, chin tucked down) that he would have to cut his fishing short and head for shore. He never complained, he never refused to take her along, but his disappointment on such nights hung in the air, palpable, like the whine of insects.

Tonight was warm, and there was little wind. In the past, these were the nights when she would end up cold because she was tricked by the onshore heat. Now, however, she made sure to wear jeans, socks, and sweaters. When you got away from the land there was a different climate. Her father stopped rowing. He baited his hook carefully and then cast. Now was the best time, before the first fish bit. Her senses were alert, her fingers alive to every movement on her line. She thought she could detect the subtle probing of a fish mouth at her bait, testing it. Her father had once told her that he could feel the ripple of a fish approaching, its halt at the hook. Maybe he could even feel it treading water, taking time to decide. The fish around here had generations of hooks in their memory. Still, they bit. It was like those primitive people who never connected sex with babies. You'd think, after a while, they'd figure it out.

Something took her line. She tensed, fighting her excitement. Her father seemed to get slower when he pulled in a fish, testing it, working with it so as not to lose the line or the fish. She glanced at him. He smiled, his mouth clamped shut. She could tell by the lines around his eyes—those filigrees of skin that all the people had from the sun— that he was happy for her. He wouldn't speak. She suspected that his silences on the water were almost a magical belief in invisibility. Fish would bite anything, so they obviously couldn't *see*, but did they hear?

She nodded at Wen and pulled slowly, patiently. But she lost it.

There were hours ahead, so she tried not to be disappointed. Even if they caught nothing, and when had that ever happened?, it was still a good feeling. She was close to her father because of these nights. They were wrapped together in the dark and the water like unborn twins.

The moon was sinking lower, and it cast broad shadows from their boat. They looked like a castle—she and her father the towers—on some vast moat.

She felt it when Wen's line pulled taut and gripped her own rod sympathetically.

He hauled it in slowly, and she could feel the weight, a good size, before it slapped into his hands.

Her father held it, taking out the hook. He glanced at it quickly, then slipped it back in the water. She eyed him questioningly, and he shrugged lightly, just a suggestion at the shoulders.

There must have been something odd about it. Her father always threw back deformed fish, those with one eye, with a ripped fin, with a fungus at the gills. He wanted only perfect things, or his sympathies were aroused by losses. Someday she would have to ask.

The moon was so low it ran a ladder on the water. Her father cast into the ladder, moving with a slight ripple. He pulled slightly on the line, then slightly again. Rachel could see his line snag. Her father tugged thoughtfully, and his motions became very delicate, as if he were testing a bruise. Rachel stared into the water. She could tell what her father was thinking just as if he said it out loud. "What's this? Caught? On what? Too high to be a lobster trap. No marking for a buoy. A bag of garbage just below the surface? Possibly that."

If it were garbage, then he could save his hook and lure. He lifted one hand to the oar. Rachel's line was on the other side of the boat; she could leave it there without any problem if they moved.

Her father didn't like losing hooks, so she figured she knew what he would do. But even if it was a foregone conclusion, he would take the moment to weigh his actions. Then, as she anticipated, he dipped one oar into the water, and they slowly revolved straight into the ladder, climbing up to the third rung.

Wen's fingers followed the line into the water, breaking the surface, which shimmered giddily for a second. His arm was clear in the moonlight as it searched deeper along the line. She felt his surprise at whatever he'd found, the way his busy fingers crept along whatever it was, deciphering its form. He leaned lower, and Rachel automatically leaned the other way to steady the boat.

She was tempted to ask him what it was. But she decided not to; once her father knew, she would know. He would nod to himself, and she would understand.

Clearly, he thought he could get the hook because he continued to probe under the surface. He was lower now, his shoulder in the water, his ear almost on the surface, as if listening.

There was a sudden shift, almost unnoticeable, it was so graceful. Leaning far over to balance the boat, Rachel saw a look of surprise on her father's face, a gaping glance at her, and then he was pulled into the water, so silently it was like a trick he'd long planned on producing, as if he'd finally found the moment when it was right.

He didn't even splash her. She stretched her arms out to steady the boat and then scurried over to his side.

The ladder was swinging. She blinked, glancing quickly at the moon. It would set soon. She swept her hands into the water, as if she could clear it away. Her fingers caught on strands of something, and she jerked back.

She grabbed an oar, sweeping it into the water. She had to find him. The water had a thick consistency to it, and the oar had trouble. She pulled it out—straight out and up—and used it to push the boat closer up the ladder. She peered intently, searching for Wen. Her heart was beating very fast, and she could see a shape about a foot below. She reached down and grabbed it. Wen's hand closed on hers, and she pulled with all her might. There were webs surrounding him, webs of colossal weight. She held onto him with one hand, and with the other frantically tried clearing the net. It *was* a net, a huge net, folding back and forth in on itself. She was convinced that if she could find the edge, she could clear it away.

She pulled at Wen, scrabbling around him to find the net. No matter how much she pulled, there was more. But Wen's hand was above the water now. She bent down, searching for his head, following his arm to the elbow. She pulled and pulled, straining her feet against the seat of the boat, calculating how much she could move without capsizing. She couldn't afford to lose the boat; it gave her the only solid yield.

She could see her father's face. His eyes were open, looking at her, pleading. His lips were moving as if he would speak. She was wildly anxious to know what he was saying. Was he telling her what to do?

A piece of the net rolled back on him and covered his face. She held onto his hands as the tide moved, pulling him away. The boat moved with her. Her feet were curled around the seat; she was straddled on her stomach now to steady them all: boat, father, self.

The ladder was breaking up. A sudden lip of light crept down to Wen's face. He was still speaking, or was it a trace of net across his chin that moved, white and sibilant, like a mouth?

With a startled cry she felt his hand relax and move away. It was like a farewell, the way it just gave up.

The ladder was falling apart as Wen's hand swept down. She scrambled for the flashlight, peering left and right. On the surface now, licking up and down, were terrible strands of the net. She swept her flashlight around, probing the floor of the boat for the knife. When she found it she began cutting at the web, but it took both hands. The net was tough plastic.

She pushed her oar against it to move, always sensing where her father would be, under the surface, rolling up in his shroud, until finally the net began to edge down, disappearing, and she knew she had lost.

She wept. Her shoulders bowed down, her hands clutching the sides of the boat, she sobbed in great shattering bursts that eventually shocked her into silence. Wiping her face on her sweater, she looked despondently again at the water. She stared and drifted, and finally a thought occurred to her, a thought that developed into a certainty. What she'd seen just couldn't be true. Her father had swum to shore—was, even now, swimming—or had been hauled on board by some other fisherman, astonished at what came out of the sea, or it had been a joke, one that baffled her, but a joke nonetheless.

She took up the oars and pulled. People don't die like that, in silence; she'd never heard of it happening. In a storm, yes. Of disease, yes. Murdered, suicide, yes. But pulling a hook out of a net? Fishing calmly, touching the tip of the water? No. There was a mistake here; she was willing to recognize a mistake.

She paused, lifting the oars out of the water. Should she stay where she was? Would her father expect her to wait? She let the oars drop and pulled again. He would head for shore, she knew it. She could see him shaking his head, a rueful look on his face when she confessed, finally, to thinking about wailing for him. In the dark? With all that water? What did she think he was, radar? He would swim for the lights of shore.

She pulled in, smiling at her own foolishness. But her smile was stretched too tight, she could feel that it wouldn't relax.

Carefully, composedly, she placed the oars neatly on the seats and tugged the boat ashore, checking twice that its ties were secure. She brushed herself off. She took up the bait box and the rods and then, thinking, put them back.

She walked over to the lights of the tavern. Her father—cold and wet and fished out of the sea—would still insist on a glass of beer, on treating whoever caught him and took him ashore, or telling, in words well chosen and frugal like expensive seeds, what it could cost a man to retrieve a hook. She stepped up to the lighted window and peered inside. Four tables, three chairs around each. The bar itself, polished wood with bowls of salted peanuts. Stools with ripped maroon vinyl. Five men, five glasses in front of them. Not one of them her father. She watched patiently, straining to hear if anyone talked of her father, straining to see if anyone emerged from the back, a borrowed towel rubbing his face. They talked of fish. They talked of boats. And no one emerged from the back.

Of course he would have gone home, she told herself. To change his clothes. To find his daughter. If it wasn't some elaborate joke, and even if it was, then he would want to make sure she was safe.

She bolted half the way home, her heart thumping. When she turned up the street to her house, though, she slowed down, catching her breath. She shut her eyes and stopped. "I'll see him there," she thought, "and he'll be laughing. He'll tell me I was a fool to worry, and he'll smile. And for his birthday I'll buy him a hundred fishhooks, so he'll never have to go after another one again." She crossed her fingers and wished it to be true. Then she strolled up to the house, telling herself she needn't hurry. She circled the house once, not very closely, her ears perked for the sound of his voice, his cough, or her mother's voice, talking to him, scolding him for his wet clothes.

She thought she did hear voices and looked into the living-room window. Her mother was ironing a shirt. Next to her were ironed shirts on hangers, dresses on hangers. A tablecloth was folded neatly on the table. The TV was on, its gray-and-white face flashing onto her mother's hands, the voices of people in their rightful places talking to each other, a sound track egging them on. A woman spoke and a man answered. Rachel watched as her mother's arm ran back and forth over a sleeve, as she leaned forward, frowning, and turned the dial. She rested the iron at the end of the board, ran a palm over her forehead, looked at her watch. Rachel moved away as her mother came to the window and squinted into the shadows, down the street. She saw nothing. No doubt she knew she would see nothing. Rachel hid in the shadows. A sickeningly vivid scene played in Rachel's mind, in gray and white like the TV: Rachel appearing at the door, a brief question—"Where's your father?"—and her mother's scream, a terrible thing to hear, even in imagination. Rachel turned away, feeling sick She crept into the shadows, and when her mother went back to ironing, she crept down the streets, afraid to meet anyone, afraid someone might stop her and ask, "How's your father, then?"

She picked her way carefully back to the boat and took the flashlight stowed under the seat. One minute she believed her father was dead, and the next minute she thought he was, even now, swimming toward shore, lifting himself out of the water, walking along the harbor. She shone her flashlight on the ground, looking for wet footprints. She walked down to the quay, circled back to the tavern, her mouth clamped shut, mute tears on her face. She kept seeing her father's face in that water, seeming to tell her something. What was it? Was he telling her where to meet him, where to search for him? Shame washed over her for not understanding.

Once she saw something white flapping at the edge of the water, and she was afraid it was her father's arm. When she got closer, she saw it was a dead fish, nothing more, but its stomach was shredded and peeling, and the sight of that sickened her again.

She couldn't go home, she knew that; it was impossible to go home without him.

Lights were going off all over town. She felt that she was losing time, that she had to find him before it was all completely dark She peered in windows, listened at doors. No one's voice was alarmed, no one mentioned her father. She didn't feel free to enter any house, ask for help, disclose her secret, admit that she'd lost her father, watched him die, pulled slowly out of her reach. Once she said it, it might be true.

The last men were shuffling home; even the bar was closing. Keeping close to the shadows, Rachel followed them, listening to snatches of conversation. "And then he said, ... " but none of the people mentioned mattered to her.

She was still out of sight, hidden by a doorway, when her mother's voice broke into their talk. "I'm looking for Wen and Rachel," she said. "Have you seen them?" Her voice had an anxious ring to it and sounded almost foreign.

The men said their various noes.

"They went fishing," her mother went on, "hours ago."

"Yes, it's late," one man said abruptly. "And the weather's good for tomorrow. He should be back."

"Maybe he stopped off for a drink?" her voice pleaded meekly.

"Bar's closed."

Rachel heard their shifting feet on the pavement. The idea of bed appealed to the men, but there was a hidden request in her mother's voice.

"We'll walk down to the boats with you," a man finally decided, and the hesitations suddenly disappeared.

Rachel slipped behind them, too far to hear anything other than the pattern of their words, her mother's voice rising and falling, the men's voices washing around it gently and soothingly.

Rachel took a side street and ran on the balls of her feet to the dock, hulking down low and hiding among the tarps and discarded buoys. She wanted to be close enough, but not too close; to hear and not to be seen.

Someone had gotten a flashlight and swept its tube of light over the rowboats gathered on shore.

"That's it," her mother said, relieved. "That's his boat."

"All right then. He's got nowhere to go but home now."

Rachel pictured her father's face, his lips moving. She closed her eyes and clutched herself.

"We'll walk you back then," the man said agreeably, and they turned, their voices dipping up and down, gay and not a little smug, thinking of Wen blinking in surprise when the search party took his wife home.

Rachel, not even bothering to wipe off the sand that stuck to her legs and lined the inside of her shoes, crept after them. She watched, again, from the outside, as they all went inside the house, the men shifting their legs inside the door as her mother called out, "Wen?" She watched as her mother went from room to room, turning on lights, each call of "Wen?" hitting a higher note.

"Perhaps he's hurt," the men suggested. "An accident down one of the streets."

"We came the way he would come."

"I'll get more lights and call a few others. We'll find him." A man's rough hand patted her mother's shoulder. "You should stay here in case he comes."

"I can't stay here," she said firmly, opening drawers for flashlights, quickly reaching for things she might need. Rachel knew her mother's practical bent, but she couldn't make out the objects: scissors, bandages, aspirin? Would she leave a sign pinned to the door, just in case, "Gone looking for you"?

Lights were beginning to go on in other houses. Rachel stepped back into the bushes, picking away the branches that clung to her sweater, making herself small. She watched the men leave, and her mother leave, heard knocking on doors, voices calling, windows raised, and quick flashes of words, "Who's there? What? I'll be right down."

They were spreading out, walking in twos and threes, shining their lights in the corners, swinging in back of trees and bushes. Rachel moved behind them, judging a safe distance, but once she tripped over a loose stone, and the lights ahead of her stopped as someone whispered, "Ssst! Hear that? What is it?"

It was now impossible for her to step forward. She expected if they found her, their hands would snap at her face, clutch at her hair. She might have welcomed that, but she couldn't stand the thought of her mother's eyes.

She backed away slowly, careful not to make a sound. She went up the hill, where the houses thinned out and the twisted, wind-bent trees pointed up to the summit. The first night she looked back down to the traces of light like fireflies in the town, imagining the sounds. By the second night she had passed over to the other side of the ridge, walking inland where there were no more sounds of the sea and no smells of fish, where it was hard to imagine water so vast it could hide a man, and where no one's lips told her things she couldn't understand.

One Spectacular God

Uncle Maury was a loving and unassuming man, especially when it came to his favorite niece, Kim. He felt a special kind of friendship with her, a peaceful delight in her responses, in her childish triumphs and achievements.

Maury admired the fresh way Kim attacked each day; she had an absolute lust for life. Her favorite game was to catch sight of an adult, let out a joyous yell, then run at them shrieking madly, jumping wildly into their arms. Most of the men and some of the women would swirl her around, her legs around their waists, her eyes closed in bliss, and her mouth wide open in that caroling yell. When he heard it, for an instant, Maury remembered exactly how it felt to be a child, to believe in everything.

Kim was six years old, an age when her mind ran almost as fast as her legs. Her two brothers, Jed, ten, and Davey, nine, scoffed at playing with her and liked it when the family dog, Bootleg, knocked Kim down, placing his great paws on her shoulders and licking her face. Kim no longer cried when she found herself sprawled on the ground with Bootleg's large head blinking at her. Crying made matters worse, for Davey was quick to point out that *he* never cried and that she was just a baby after all.

At times of such frustration, Kim turned to her uncle, who lived three houses down. He was a pudgy and beaming man with soft pink hands and eyebrows that constantly darted up and down. He was an amateur magician and counted on Kim for an uncritical audience. Jed and Davey had had their turns at applauding him but Jed, and then Davey, had outgrown Uncle Maury's magic. Some day Kim would too, but Maury held no grudge about it. He loved them each, and he loved the sheer fact of their growing, even as it separated them.

Of course, at the age of six Kim was far from perfect. She wasn't a good eater, for example, although her mother was a good cook who made full dinners, no matter how hot it was—roasts and mashed potatoes and a bowl of vegetables.

One time Jed was passing the bowl of mashed potatoes over to Davey, and Kim was sitting between them. Her head fell with perfect accuracy into the bowl of potatoes. Jed pulled Kim out, still sleeping, by the hair on her head, and Davey yelped, "I didn't even have mine yet!" while their mother split her sides laughing and apologizing: "I'm sorry, I'm sorry, I didn't even see her yawn!" She got up for a washrag while Davey furiously scooped clots of potato off Kim's face, making unpleasant noises. "She's just a wind-up doll after all," their mother said fondly, wiping Kim's face before carrying her up to bed, "and she winds down all at once."

Maury was at their table so often that the family seemed to consist of three children, three adults. Or, when Kim's mother was annoyed with Maury, three-and-a-half children, two-and-a-half adults. Kim had heard her mother complain about Maury and his strange notions. "Maury's at it again," she said to Kim's father. "He says he's going to quit his job and devote himself to magic. Magic!" Her voice clanged dismissively.

Kim couldn't tell why her mother would be annoyed with this, and she shied away from asking because of the tone of her voice. But the next time she saw Uncle Maury she asked him what his regular job was.

"I sell notions," he said. "You know, buttons and ribbons and zippers and frogs."

"Frogs?"

"People put them on their coats," he said absently.

Kim chewed her lip. "Do they like that?" she asked, about the frogs.

"Oh, they like it all right," he said about the people, "but it's not much in fashion, these days."

Kim thought, gravely, that it shouldn't be the fashion, ever. Her mother had told her that frogs needed to be kept wet. Although maybe, she thought haltingly, maybe people put them on raincoats.

"Uncle Maury," she said suddenly, not wanting to think about frogs anymore, "I think I've got a tingle in my ear." She smiled at him, and Uncle Maury chuckled back.

"Your ear?" he said. "Not that again?" His broad hand shifted quickly from his jacket and approached her head. "Is it your right ear this time?" His fingers brushed against her hair, and he jumped slightly back. "What?" he cried. "What's this?" He held a quarter out in front of her as she giggled. "You'll never be a poor girl, Kim, with ears like *that.*"

She quivered with delight. "I've lost my hankie," she said. "Did you find it?"

A look of grave concern spread across his face as he mumbled, "I know I saw it somewhere," and began to pat his pockets and all his hiding places (even his socks) until he looked finally in the cuff of his jacket. "This could be something," he said seriously, and plucked at a little corner of cloth poking out. The handkerchiefs came out, hand in hand, first white and then pink and then red, a whole rainbow of them, as Kim grabbed the first one Uncle Maury handed her and leaped around the room.

She never tired of any of his tricks; half her delight consisted simply in knowing which trick it would be, in being instrumental in producing it. She knew that quarters only appeared when Uncle Maury was around, but, again, they always came out of *her* ears.

One day Uncle Maury was practicing some routines for a show he was planning when she sneezed, and he automatically said, "God bless you." Kim asked, "Who's God?" She had already asked a few people that question and had not succeeded in grasping the answer. Her mother had said that God was the person who created absolutely everything, even Kim, even Mommy. Kim, however, remembered what she had been told when she'd asked where babies came from, and she got confused. Her mother ended by saying, "God is like energy, like magic, like light from a lightbulb. You get the lightbulb from a store, don't you? But you don't get light from a store." She trailed off uncertainly. "I'm not explaining it right. I don't know how you describe God, it's the kind of thing it takes a long time to get an idea about. Ask me again, okay?"

But instead she asked Uncle Maury, who bit his lip and shoved a rabbit back into a hat and thought out loud. "God? That's a hard one. Behind everything you don't understand, there's God. And behind all the beautiful things, too." He laughed at himself. "That's no help, is it? Well, you have to start with a very small thing—let's see, like this button on your dress. Now imagine the button is very big, like a house. Now imagine it's even bigger, like the sky. And then bigger again, like all the sky you can't even see. That's God. And then imagine a minute. Just so big. But do the same thing with a minute that you did with a button, until you can't imagine it, and that's God, too. Only you have to do that with everything, you see, because God is behind everything. At least, that's what I understand." He looked at her face, which was solemn and impressed. "It takes a long time to figure out what God means. So I've been told. But look here, do you see this rope? How many pieces do you see? Well, I bet I can cut one in half and still have the same number of ropes. Want to see?"

Kim nodded her head and watched her uncle hold the ropes in his hand, cut one, and then show her exactly the same number of pieces.

"Did you do that, or did God do that?" she asked after he finished. "I did it," Uncle Maury said proudly.

"Then what does God do?"

"God makes everything out of nothing," her uncle sighed. "Don't you like my trick?"

"The cards," she said. "Please show me the cards."

"You don't like *new* tricks," Uncle Maury said wisely. "You like the tricks where you know what's coming, don't you? They're like old friends to you."

And Uncle Maury did the trick where he pretended to lose a deck of cards, only to pick them, fan after fan, out of the air. Kim loved the expression on her uncle's face—the open mouth, the eyes bulging with surprise—as time after time he whipped his hand into the air and swept out more cards.

"There seem to be more cards than usual," he said finally. "Where are they coming from?" The spilled cards mounted up on the table.

"More cards, Uncle Maury!" Kim cried, gleefully shaking her head. Both she and Uncle Maury heard the coin drop onto the bare wood floor. Kim squealed and picked it up as the last spray of cards fell from her uncle's hands.

Uncle Maury opened Kim's hand. "Where did that come from?" he asked.

Kim smiled, thinking this was another trick. "It fell from my ear," she said proudly. "It's *my* quarter."

"Of course it's yours," he said gallantly. He checked his pockets for holes, but found none.

"I'll never be poor," Kim chortled.

"You'll never be poor," Uncle Maury agreed gently. He thought perhaps he was getting absentminded; he didn't remember taking out the coin. He was either getting absentminded or very, very good.

Uncle Maury did not really intend to quit selling notions in order to do magic; that was Kim's mother's fantasy. He liked his job; he liked handling finery and strange, small shapes. The objects in his display box pleased him, and he liked to take them out, handle them, show them to his customers. He liked the barrel-shaped buttons and the filigree hooks that fit intricately into their eyes. The way he appreciated his own merchandise, the courtesy with which he handled it, prompted most of his sales. Maury's respect was contagious; his customers could *see* the possibilities of a lace collar when Maury held it; it was only later, ignored below a glass counter, that the collar became questionable, outdated, and somehow suspect. Without Maury, his notions seemed to grow limp.

Kim's mother pretended to see magic as a threat because she distrusted enthusiasm. For years she had been anticipating Maury's downfall, not out of animosity but out of lack of belief. So much goodwill and innocent pride was bound to result in disaster. Her sympathy was always ready, and always thwarted. Maury continued with his pleasures.

The whole town was preparing for a Fourth of July talent show. The local hardware store, part of a massive chain, was sponsoring a day-long celebration, culminating in a fireworks display. The high school band was performing, the local dance school was putting on a display, as were the piano teacher and her students, the local gym and its tumblers. There would even be a dog show (Jed and Davey were showing Bootleg). Uncle Maury had signed up as soon as the first rumors had circulated. He was listed on the poster.

As the weather grew hot in mid-June, he found it harder and harder to practice for long stretches with his top hat, his tailcoat, his vest with the hidden pockets. He was not an inspired magician; he never created his own tricks, and he needed wires up his sleeve, fake thumbs, hidden pockets. He perspired too much, it made his getup ridiculous, but he couldn't bear to part with the tricks he knew. He felt he was a slow learner, and every trick required a built-in prop.

Kim came to visit in shorts, scuffed sandals with white socks, little halters, squatting on the floor as Uncle Maury huffed his way through the routine. He kept one eye on her, judging her reaction when he threw in a joke, a new bit of patter. It occurred to him once, as she gazed at him with her serious gray eyes, that he was aiming his whole act at a six-year-old, and then he raced to his set of *The Tarbell Course in Magic*. He really should try to add something more adult.

By late June the children were getting restless, fighting over how to groom the dog and how to show him, pulling and tugging from opposite sides. They were impossible, terrible, quick-tempered, sniping. More than once, Jed and Davey and Kim were consigned to the living room: "You sit there, and you sit there, and you sit *there,* and I don't want to hear another peep out of any of you!" their mother yelled, her hair all disordered, as if she'd been pulling it. This worked for a while, three hostile pairs of eyes roaming around the room restlessly, guarding three clenched mouths. But then Jed or Davey would stick his tongue out, and Kim would cross her eyes, their fidgeting breaking out in dramatic clusters, as they squirmed and flicked like garden hoses let loose, enough to drive anyone crazy.

They were punished so often the last two weeks before Independence Day that Kim's mother believed she would go mad ("What can I do? Strap them into chairs and tape their mouths? They'd still keep *moving!"*), and Uncle Maury had plenty of time for uninterrupted practice of his new trick. He was going to saw a person in half!

He rubbed his hands gleefully, going over and over the instructions in his book. He constructed the boxes himself and attached wheels to the bottom and hinges to the side.

He was also practicing making things disappear, which required a very large cloth and a very quick hand. He had progressed to the point where he could handle glasses and bottles and plates; he was working on a bread box when Kim poked her head in.

He motioned to her. "Come in, come in. I've almost got it." He lifted a bread box onto the table. "New trick, Kim. Watch and see."

Kim sat down, waiting patiently.

"See this bread box, lovely thing. Had it in the family for years," Uncle Maury began. "I'd really hate to let go of this now, it's an antique."

"Antique," Kim echoed cheerfully, startling Uncle Maury. She associated the word with magic from then on.

He continued his talk until the point where he said, "Now you see it, now you don't! Well, that happens with bread, why not a bread box?" and he whipped the cloth away, showing an empty table.

Kim laughed. "I closed my eyes," she said. "I didn't see it."

Uncle Maury sighed. "There's nothing *to* see, Kim. It's gone. I made it disappear."

"Oh." Kim licked her lip, and her hand started to wander to her ear. "Uncle Maury?"

"Now wait," he said hastily, "I want to show you one more thing before I give—er, before your ear—well, just wait. Where's my top hat?" He swept around the room quickly. "I want to show you how—"

"You made it disappear, Uncle Maury," Kim said. "It was right next to the bread box."

"Was it?" Uncle Maury said thoughtfully and bent down below the table. His head popped up again, flushed. "No. Not there. You must be mistaken."

"I saw it. I know I did," Kim said with absolute conviction.

"All right, all right," he said, mumbling to himself. "What kind of magician can make things disappear and then can't find them? It must be the heat."

He worked patiently at his disappearances. The heat increased, and he pulled distractedly at the pink-and-red hankies up his sleeve, using them to wipe his brow. They trailed after him like a loyal dog as he walked back and forth, rehearsing his jokes, controlling his moves.

"Play dead, Bootleg," Davey yelled. Bootleg's ears flattened; he lowered his head to the ground, then rolled over slowly on his back and let his legs dangle in the air, bent at the wrist.

"I hate that!" Kim squealed. "Don't make him dead again!" Her face got red and hot; she stomped her feet. "Okay, Bootleg!" she yelled. The dog scrambled to his feet, and Davey pushed Kim down.

He stuck his tongue out. "Go away. We don't want you here! You're ruining our trick! You're ruining it!"

Kim stamped her feet, in order not to cry. They were always complaining about her. And then an idea came to her, and she turned and ran to her uncle. She would show Davey and Jed.

"Uncle Maury," she cried, flushed and perspiring, her face smudged from one of Bootleg's licks, "Uncle Maury, I want to be one of your tricks." "Umm?" Uncle Maury said, frowning. He was powdering a deck of cards—"the invisible deck," one of his newest tricks. Unfortunately he didn't think it would show well in an auditorium. He was beginning to worry about the quality of his performance. Surely, in a small town, they wouldn't expect much? And surely he should give them more than they'd expect? He longed to startle them, to awe them. It would be a pleasure to make Kim's mother gasp, to make them all gasp. Kim used to applaud his magic, when he first started, but a kind of expectant consumerism soon overtook her, and it seemed she now deserved his tricks, like supper.

He studied Kim, frowning. Most magicians had a leggy female assistant who shuffled boxes, set up props, and proved with predetermined moves that, indeed, there were no strings.

He didn't know any such young women, and besides, they would probably be taller than he was.

But Kim. It would be a nice touch to have her in the act. Innocence. A suggestion of almost God-like honesty. "Well, yes," he said, thinking rapidly. "That's a good idea." He eyed her thoughtfully. "Can you be quiet and keep very still if I ask you to?"

"Of course I can," Kim said, injured. "I'm a big girl now."

"You are," he agreed. "How would you like to disappear?"

She sucked on her lip for a moment. "Like the bread box?"

He nodded.

"Is that all?"

"Well," he hesitated, "how would you like to be cut in half?"

Her nose wrinkled. "Does it hurt?"

"Not a bit. It doesn't even tickle."

"Then I'll do it," she said solemnly.

Uncle Maury smiled happily. "We'll get you a costume," he said. "All in white. I have lace collars, bits of satin. Your mother can make it. Or someone." He went in search of his samples, picking out last year's suitcase with the discontinued lines. Caps and frills, tucks and fichus, embroidered hankies, furbelows, tatted scarves. They ranged from white to ecru.

"Dress up!" Kim trilled.

"Yes, yes, you'll look very fine. Like a star, like an angel, like a picture in a book."

And she did look ethereal. Against all predictions, she did not scrape her knees or scar her face or gash her arm before the performance. She learned her movements, only occasionally getting distracted and needing reminders ("Oh, Kim, will you do *that* when everyone's watching?"). She jerked upright, still as a board, her bright eyes intent and out of focus as she went through her internal checklist. She was going to show Davey and Jed; she was going to show them all.

July Fourth dawned hot and brilliant. The dog show was in the park at noon. Davey and Jed pulled Bootleg, panting and drooling, into the ranks of the other dogs. He had a tendency to collapse the minute their attention wandered, sprawling out under a tree or crawling under the bandstand. Their mother had given them a huge juice jar of water and warned them about the heat. Jed was frantic, caught between his love for Bootleg and his dreams of stealing the show. He dripped water on the dog's head to keep him cool, producing an effect not unlike a wet sweater. And then he jerked Bootleg's collar and commanded him to sit *up* or sit *down.*

Bootleg shuffled up when it was his turn and he patiently offered his paw when told to shake hands, got up on his hind legs and begged, rolled over and sighed when told to play dead. Both Davey and Jed were scarlet with excitement; Jed's freckles seemed to form a textured mask across the beet red of his skin. But Bootleg didn't win after all. That honor went to Riches, a wire-haired terrier who could jump over backwards three times in a row. Jed burst into tears with disappointment.

The magic show started in the late afternoon. The auditorium doors and windows were kept open because of the heat, and fitful little bursts of air crept through and rippled the cloth on Uncle Maury's table.

"Kim," Uncle Maury hissed unhappily, his hands damp, "you remember what to do? If you forget anything, just say, 'What now, magician?' and I'll tell you, okay? Say it!" His eyes were large and startled, and he licked his lips.

"What now, magician?" Kim piped. She liked the way it sounded and repeated it again.

"That's good, that's good," he said, realizing too late that she might like to say it for no reason at all.

But everything started well. He and Kim came out on stage hand in hand, Kim in her patchwork dress of white and ecru, lace and crewel, Uncle Maury in his cape and top hat. Kim sat on a folding chair next to him while Uncle Maury did his opening routines. He released doves into the air, he made a wand float all around him, even behind him, he poured milk into a glass that was much too small and still the glass was empty.

People came and went during the performance, but, even so, Uncle Maury was gratified to see that the auditorium was filling up. The scuffle and rasp of chairs was as pleasant as applause.

Kim sat patiently at first, waiting for her cue. But once, as Uncle Maury fumbled at his table, arranging his props, she glanced quickly around the room and called out, "What now, magician?" An appreciative ripple spread through the rows, disconcerting Uncle Maury. He quickly took her into the act, pulling out a deck of cards. "Pick a card, any card," he said, turning to her.

She stood next to him formally and picked a card.

Uncle Maury, of course, knew which card it was; it was one of his special decks. But the funny thing was, he could *see* the card. He had a miniature mental image of it right in his forehead between his eyes, just above his nose. He could have laid his finger on the exact spot.

The picture in his forehead excited him and he daringly sent Kim out to the audience with the deck. "Pick a card!" Kim chirped, and people obliged, smiling and nudging each other as Maury called it out. He was the only one surprised by his accuracy, by what was happening in his forehead. He couldn't stop doing it. He could see the card in the audience with his eyes closed, with his back turned; the cards teased him on and on. He was in danger of boring his audience, unaware that feet were shifting restlessly, chairs rattling and scraping backwards. It was the same thing, over and over again.

But Kim understood what all this rustling and clearing of throats meant. "What now, magician?" she demanded.

Maury frowned, suddenly catching the mood of the audience. Kim came back with the cards. He took them, swept them around him to show the audience, and then they were gone.

It was one of his favorite tricks, the one, in fact, that had first caused him to turn to magic. The cards were gone and yet, with a pluck into the air, there was a fan of cards, another spray of cards. He dropped them on the floor, allowing them to pile up as he pulled more from the air, and more, and more, until his eyebrows knitted, and the audience sat forward on their chairs. He had the picture in his forehead again, even when by rights there should be no more cards, when there could *not* be any more cards. Yet he pulled them from the air, bouquets of cards, ranks of cards, complete runs of cards so that they piled around his feet and his breathing grew fast. Never in his life had anything been so perfect. Never in his life had anything been so pure and easy, so blissful, so powerful and sweet.

A round of applause broke out, and he pulled them, faster and faster, until the applause died out and he was bathed in sweat, glassy-eyed and numb. He could have fanned more cards, he knew, but his arms ached and his heart was drumming and abruptly he stopped, showing the front and back of his hands, twirling them around as a single last card fell out and fluttered to the pile on the floor. What else was he capable of? His head was clear and sharp, almost brittle. He sensed that he could do more, he could do anything, yet it was more than a sense, it was a bright, illuminated confidence in the gift itself.

People were standing at the back of the auditorium now; there were few vacant seats.

"What now, magician?" Kim prompted as Uncle Maury stood staring at the pile of cards at his feet. The little hairs on his skin seemed to stand up, he was so conscious of himself, of this odd state of himself. He was a great magician, he knew; his fantasy was come alive. He glanced at Kim. She was enjoying herself. She could feel the goodwill of the audience toward her. And she knew so many of Uncle Maury's tricks that she could be excused for feeling in command sometimes, watching with an almost adult pride as he produced yet another miracle. Maury might be surprised; she was not.

And then suddenly, someone in the middle of the auditorium sneezed. Kim giggled and her eyes lit up, and she said, "Do you have a hankie, magician?" She reached her hand out to Uncle Maury's cuff and he pulled on the pointed tip of a red nylon handkerchief, and then Kim skipped off across the stage to the stairs that led to the auditorium, down to the middle row, where she stopped, gazing down the line of faces. She looked at Uncle Maury, who stood center stage, his arm slightly raised, and from his wrist there was a stream of red, pink, white hankies, alternating with strict regularity—yards and yards of them, so many that Kim was seized with a whimsical wish to pull and pull the bright chain of them. She took off with a double skip to the back of the auditorium where she took a tum behind the last row until it came to an end, and she turned again, racing up to the stage.

Cheerfully, the audience at the turns helped keep the hankies from catching, they laughed and smiled as the bouncing line wound around them once, and then Kim began another circuit, and more people reached out laughing and passed the line along. They watched Kim; they nudged each other; they weren't the least bit amazed at the impossible number of hankies being pulled from Uncle Maury's sleeve. The line of hankies wrapped the auditorium once, twice, three times, until everyone in the seats at the end of the row—and the whole first and last rows—had arms reaching out, eyes judging the next patch of pink or red or white to be grabbed, when Kim changed course and raced back up to the stage and panting, cried, "What next, magician?"

At that, Uncle Maury dropped his arm and the last hankie fell out.

A round of applause burst out from the audience. Offstage, a scratchy, unrecognizable recording began to play. Kim bowed as the next act, a family of acrobats, began its first tumbles across the stage. Uncle Maury picked up his table and crept offstage, stunned.

His eyes stung with tears. He had never done magic before, he had only done tricks. He looked at his hands and turned them around, hoping to see something, anything to confirm that there was a new and permanent quality to them. All around him the amateur show went on, as if nothing remarkable had happened out there, as if his performance had gone quite as expected, and not further. No one had noticed the touch of greatness. Carefully, he packed his props away and folded his table. Then he opened his bag again, took out a fresh deck, and palmed five cards. Mouthing his words, he went through his routine and five cards appeared and five cards were flung down—but five cards only.

Outside he found Kim showing off in front of her brothers as crowds of people began to move purposefully to the center of the fairgrounds. The fireworks would begin in fifteen minutes.

Kim raced up to him, clutching her ear. "Uncle Maury, it itches! What could it be?"

Distracted, he reached his hand forward, and pulled out nothing. She looked at him, stunned. He quickly snuck his other hand into his pocket and with overdone surprise claimed, "Why, Kim! It was in your other ear all along!"

He took Kim's hand as her brothers went in search of their parents, and his legs moved automatically. He was a modest man, far too unassuming to think he could despair; he had never really wanted anything enough to be worthy of despair. But he began to feel an insult or injury that seemed impossibly remote. How could he explain what had happened? His feet moved on and his hand clutched Kim, and it began to seem to him that the mysteries in life did not necessarily exist because of hidden plans; maybe they were there out of a kind of carelessness. Maybe God (or whatever there might be behind it all) had dropped that moment of excellence, without warning or forethought, like an overlooked crumb from a table. And with that crumb Maury could have done anything, anything. If only he'd had time to think, what might he have done? He'd had one chance, and he alone knew he had been extraordinary, a magician who made illusions into reality. Did such things ever happen twice?

When the first aerial bomb burst, he held Kim's hand so tight that she complained. When the second bloomed, blue and pink in the air, he picked her up and her legs climbed his waist. Her head leaned back as the clusters broke out: spangled, dappled, bursting, dying.

The sky split open around them; they could see its edges. The colors bled and then disappeared. Kim rested her head on her uncle's shoulder, and sounds rocked the country, shattering the air. The night, deep blue, dripped all around them, with luminous whites drifting down to their feet. Even now, Uncle Maury thought, even now it might be someone else's turn, and someone else's heart might be lifting up, incredulous and unambitious, in a moment of perfection too trivial for anyone else to notice.

He held onto Kim while they watched the stars spilling out of the sky.

The Light at The End

Beggars are just a fact of life, like losing your hair or getting old. Sometimes they seem to have meaning, in and of themselves, but you have to be careful with that—meanings aren't born, they're made. For instance, one morning a skinny woman in rags stood by the token booth at my subway station. She rocked back and forth, rattling a paper cup, saying, "I don't wanna go like this. Please help me someone. Please help me, please." It's the kind of thing that can stick in your head all day like your own personal chant, if you're not careful. I disliked the way she stood by the token booth, however; I gave her nothing.

During rush hour you never see a lot of beggars, but during off-hours, it's a parade of them, one after the other, shuffling, heads lowered or eyes glaring dangerously in your face. I have an acquaintance who only gives a quarter when the person is dirty (proof of homelessness) and another who only gives when the beggar is clean (and therefore redeemable). There are skinny beggars, fat beggars, beggars who chant their appeals or sing them, and those who whisper them or pass out cards. They are men and women, talking about wars and illnesses, waving their bony hands as they shout out their failures. No one believes them (or at least very few), and if anyone gives out a quarter, it is done quickly, silently, with economy of movement and a mask of mechanical indifference. Except, of course, when the beggar brings a child, which rips everyone in two. Give them money and cause a rash of mother-and-child beggars? Don't give them money and let the child starve?

My work schedule changed recently, and I now go to work an hour later, when the crowds are thinner and the beggars are out in force. They must have their favorite routes; I run into the same ones time after time. There's the one who's lost a leg, the one who's lost a job, the one with cancer, the one with a sick wife. There's the one who thinks he's funny, and who might even *be* funny, except that it would cost us a quarter. He once came through the doors (so clearly marked "Riding between cars is prohibited"), began his talk, and then saw that there was another beggar already in full harangue, the one-legged beggar who'd come back from Vietnam. The funny beggar skidded to a halt; you could see his eyebrows raise, and he stamped his foot and said, "Shit! Competition!" and then turned and went back out through the doors marked "Do Not Use This Door."

But one morning about three months ago, just as I finished reading my paper and was folding it, the doors opened and two people came in, a man and a woman. I thought they were together, but the man sat down first and the woman looked back and forth along the length of the car before seating herself next to the man, with a privacy leverage of three inches between them.

The door to the next car slid open and a clown walked through. He had on a yellow and orange striped suit with a flounce around the waist and a blue ruffled collar. He wore lace-up sneakers with varicolored paint spatters, a pair of white cotton gloves and a huge red rubber nose. He carried a bucket and an old auto horn, and he honked three times for attention. Those easily pleased smiled; the rest of us ignored him or watched with a wary eye.

"Good morning, boys and girls," he said matter-of-factly, standing at attention and shifting his unsmiling clown's face around for eye contact. "Excuse me if I ask you to spare a minute of your time. I'm collecting for the homeless, a nickel or a dime, whatever you can manage. It probably means little to you, but it can add up to a lot for people whose lives are shattered and who have nowhere to turn."

He honked his horn and raised his voice. "Check in your pockets, turn them inside out, that isn't lint, it's a piece of money, honey, and there's someone desperate to hear that money roar. A nickel, a dime, a dime or a nickel, nothing you would miss, we're not asking anyone to hurt themselves." He honked his horn. "Just do a favor, for yourself and for some stranger. Only a nickel, folks, only a nickel, you'll never miss it; put it somewhere where it'll do some good." He honked again, nodding seriously, his chin high. He began to go down the car, his silver paint pail swinging left and right. When he got to the center he suddenly put his pail down and spun around doing a little soft-shoe sequence with his horn honking, an impressive feat in a rocking train. "A nickel or a dime, a dime or a nickel," he called at the end, squeezing his fake red nose and honking his horn at the same time. He had everyone's attention, of course; you can't do a tap dance on a subway without waking people up. It was astonishing; people dug into their pockets. They smiled and dropped their quarters into his pail. I alone stood steadfast. He paused briefly in front of me, the pail swinging invitingly, but I shifted back into my seat. I saw no reason to give him a quarter just because he tooted a horn. I don't give money for decor. There are a million hard-luck stories on the subways, and I don't have a dime for all of them. I felt him waiting there in front of me, and it was a small but conscious test of willpower, but then a passenger to my right snaked his hand forward, I heard the sound of metal hitting metal, and a multicolored foot lifted away, as if lightheartedly, to harvest other coins.

As for that couple who had earlier caught my attention, I suspected her of giving two quarters, and him of all the loose change in his pocket, perhaps even a subway token mixed in. They looked self-conscious with charity. She had short, curly dark hair, lightly feathered around her ears, and brown eyes with a very wide pupil so that they seemed all one color. She was dressed in a woman's suit—brown tweed with a light line of orange in it, a jacket and straight skirt. Her rampant professionalism was muted by colored stockings that picked up the line of amber in her clothes. Her hands were rather blunt, which surprised me because her hair was so soft, but her nails were short and well-cleaned, and the broad tips of her fingers rested competently on the structured, patent-leather handbag in her lap.

He wore a double-breasted charcoal-gray suit with a black-and-white striped shirt. His hair was a little long for a conservative office, but, as soon became apparent, we all worked midtown rather than Wall Street, and it was more likely that he worked in publishing, or some sort of venture more commercial than financial. He looked like he'd been told he had a nice smile.

They wore their youth like expensive clothes.

The train pulled out of DeKalb Avenue and into the long tunnel to Manhattan. It seemed even slower than usual that morning, and wrist watches were being consulted when, with a final defiant screech, the train suddenly stopped altogether.

A man immediately got up and headed for the front car. There's always at least one person who does that, who expects to see some sort of explanation for the delay by looking out the window next to the engineer's box. The rest of us sat where we were in the last car and waited, trying to calculate if we could make it up somewhere along the line. At ten minutes we thought we might still get to work on time. At fifteen minutes we knew we couldn't. We were going to be late, and we might as well be good and late. "What do you suppose it is?" a middle-aged woman farther down the car asked of no one in particular.

"Some damn train broke down ahead, I bet," a man in a plaid jacket said.

"Third time this month." This came from an exasperated woman who couldn't keep her eyes off her watch. "Wouldn't you know? I have an appointment, too. These doctors won't take you if you're late, but you still have to pay."

Two or three heads nodded sympathetically, and there was a thoughtful silence until the first woman said, "At least they could tell you. I mean, it's the least they can do."

"It's not so bad," a man with the merest fringe of hair around his ears said. "What is it? Over seven hundred miles of tracks? The biggest subway system in the world, and it runs all the time, too."

"Yeah, I was in London once, and they stop the trains at night," the man in the plaid jacket said.

The bald man continued. "Best record in the world. Why, it's a whole city down here, all those miles of tracks and people! Millions of people each day!" He smiled winningly; he was eager to get his point across.

"You sound like you own it," the woman with the appointment said.

"Sometimes I feel like I do. I've been a train conductor for thirty years."

He looked around expectantly.

"Thirty years," the young man said. "Thirty years in one job."

"Every day it's different. You never know what's going to happen. My name's Bill, by the way." He nodded.

The young man said, "Arthur."

The young woman said, "Melanie."

Other people offered their own names. By now, no one was checking watches.

"So I can tell you, delays like this are rare, less than one percent of the time."

"What do you think happened?" Melanie asked.

"Like he said, probably a train broke down. But sometimes it's worse." He looked significantly at them all.

"Worse?"

"Suicide. People throw themselves on the tracks, you know. It happens. I'll tell you, though, it's a helluva thing to do to a person. To the engineer most of all. I've known people's nerves to be shattered. Why, one time, a friend of mine was running his train along that big curve into Lawrence Street, you know the one? He was coming along at a good speed—top of the limit, but still the limit—when he comes around the curve and all of a sudden he sees a man standing on the tracks, just standing and waiting. No time to stop, he was just twenty yards down the track My friend hit the brakes as hard as he could, and you know, just before the train hit him, that man on the tracks looked up and *smiled!*"

"He smiled," the woman with the appointment gasped.

"My friend retired, right then and there, five years early. A shattered man."

Once again everyone fell silent, uneasily this time. Bill went into a reverie, probably thinking about his shattered friend, and one by one people began to glance at the time. Arthur cleared his throat finally and said, "Thirty minutes. We've been here thirty minutes."

The man who'd gone to the front car suddenly reappeared. "Did you find anything out? Do you know what's wrong?"

"The red light. The conductor's got the red light, that's all he knows. His radio's broken."

"Can't go past a red light," Bill insisted. "So we're stuck," Arthur said.

"If only that clown would come back," Melanie smiled. "Maybe he could cheer us up."

"He used to be funnier," Bill said. "I've run into him a lot." He was obviously going to be the authority on everything. "He used to take the B and D trains all the time. Now it's the N and the R. And he doesn't laugh anymore."

"Maybe it's a sad business," Melanie offered.

"Taking people's money? That's sad, all right!"

"It's for a worthy cause."

"Think so? Think he's honest? He's not keeping it for himself?" the man in the plaid jacket asked, with the left side of his mouth raised in practiced scorn.

"You gave him money," Arthur pointed out. "We all did."

The plaid-jacket man pursed his lips. "A nickel. A nickel only."

"But I believed him," Melanie said. Her forehead was slightly puckered in concern. It lowered a feathered fringe of hair to her eyebrows; it was really rather attractive.

"I believed him too," Arthur said, turning to smile at her. She smiled back; they kept it up for two ticks of a heartbeat, and even when they stopped you could tell that they were each waiting for the other to say something, anything, again. They were alert now, and probably very disappointed when the train suddenly rumbled and began to inch its way forward.

Melanie got off with me at Fiftieth Street. Arthur leaned forward quickly and said goodbye as she rose to go. She paused, smiled, and said, "Maybe I'll see you tomorrow," then lifted her hand in a brief wave.

"Same time, same place," he smiled bravely.

I made it a point to match the time and place too. Of course, it was my regular route and my regular schedule.

By the time I saw the clown again, Arthur and Melanie had progressed past the awkward stage (sudden lunges of conversation followed by anxious silences) and sometimes read newspapers together. They stood next to each other if they couldn't find adjoining seats, and when they did sit, they were close. Their silences were comfortable.

A few weeks later, we all heard the toot of his horn as soon as the clown came through the door. The couple looked up with a smile.

"Ladies and gentlemen, boys and girls," the clown announced. "People are hungry, people are cold. What can you do about it? Just a nickel or a dime can make a difference, a dime or a nickel. Add them all together and there's food for the hungry, clothes for the cold. What a beautiful morning," he said flatly, honking his horn. "Make it a beautiful day. It would take so little and mean so much. A nickel or a dime, a dime or a nickel. People are dying."

He skipped his way forward, his pail banging someone's knee, an accident he chose to ignore. I looked at him quickly. Although the clown looked exactly the same, the tone of his voice had an aggressive edge, and his perfunctory tap dance seemed to him to be a waste of time. But half the people in the car still managed to be amused. "A nickel, a dime, a dime or a nickel," he chanted, squeaking his nose and honking his horn. "Small change, throwaway money, what can you do with it? It's pointless, it's useless for you. What can you do with it? Chump change!"

He spun around once, tilted his head to the side, and held his pail straight out. "People are dying," he said, and honked his horn once again. A lot of passengers hadn't really been listening, they were just following him with their eyes. But the words bothered them when they thought back to what he'd said, and the smiles on their faces froze. The clown seemed to sense it, because he tucked his pail under his arm, turned around, and wiggled. "Hey, lighten up, lighten up. Let's all get together and pitch in, and together we'll make a difference! Throw in a nickel and change the world!" His horn started honking raucously, and the passengers were digging into pockets for their change, feeling slightly relieved.

I could see that Arthur and Melanie had gotten past coins and each held a discreetly folded bill in their hands. The clown moved swiftly past them. I happened to be reading a paper at the time, holding it slightly to my right, since that eye is stronger. I saw him stop in front of me—or rather I saw the stripes and the pail and heard the sharp rubber bleat of his horn, and once again I knew he was aware that I was avoiding him. He hung there angrily and then moved away with an imperious step, but I believe he understood my position. After all, if I had given him a coin the first time, I would have given it from then on. But I hadn't.

From an objective point of view, Melanie and Arthur had hit it off. I overheard references to "last night" and "tonight," sure signs that they were meeting outside the subway. They were so firmly happy that even their shoes seemed glorious.

And in front of them trooped a whole array of beggars, to all of whom Melanie and Arthur gave their money without any judgment whatsoever, as if they were putting a token into a turnstile. They missed the ominous edge, the edge I thought about night and day. I have dreams, sometimes or perhaps not dreams, but long trains of thought, of ranks of beggars at the corner of my block, in the doorway of my building, reaching out, moving forward, calling all together:

We want your jobs.
We want your homes.
We want your money.

But to Melanie and Arthur, beggars were a kind of interesting wildlife. One day as we jerked and rattled through lower Manhattan, a new beggar came through the door, making his way forward. He was lean, unshaven, in dirty clothes. He carried a brown paper bag under his left elbow. His right hand was outstretched and cupped. Instead of making a general pitch, he went privately from one person to the next. "Can you help me out?" he asked. "Just anything. I'm out of work; I'm broke."

His words carried faintly to the middle of the car, where I sat in my usual place opposite Melanie and Arthur. The two lovers were whispering privately, but I saw Melanie's head raise slightly, almost distracted, and then turn back to Arthur.

They had quarters at the ready; they were always prepared with the change, handing it out smoothly, sometimes without even interrupting their talk.

But as Melanie lifted her hand, she raised her eyes and froze. I saw the color drain from her face.

"Neil?" she asked, and her voice was cracked with fear.

The beggar, too, froze. He swayed slightly, as if trying to decide whether to stay or to move away immediately. An uneven flush spread down to his neck

"Neil," Melanie repeated, this time with certainty.

"Please," he whispered, half bent over, "don't. I don't know you."

I saw Melanie's mouth drop open and then shut. Neil straightened up and began to turn away.

"Wait," Melanie said. In her impulsiveness, she dropped her quarters on the floor. Arthur bent to pick them up as she frantically opened her wallet and started emptying it out, saying, "Take this. Take it. I don't need it. I'm sorry it's all I have. Take it."

The beggar had turned away slightly by then, still indecisive, and when he didn't take the money, Melanie lunged forward and stuck it in his pocket, in his dirty jeans pocket. Arthur held the quarters in his hand; I could tell he wasn't about to touch Neil's clothes.

Neil didn't acknowledge any of this. His jaw was clenched and his lips slightly parted, and he stared stonily ahead, to my side of the car. But this was only for a fraction of a minute. He pulled himself forward and came to me, his palm outstretched. His face was still blood-red.

"Spare any change, mister?" he asked.

I gave him a dime, slowly, and he weighed it in his hand before closing his fist. He moved to the next person and opened his hand as the train pulled into the Canal Street station and the doors slid wide. He looked again at his hand, and then walked stiffly out of the train and onto the platform without once looking back at Melanie.

Her eyes never left him. I shifted slightly in my seat to get a better view, and I saw him standing on the other side of the window. He had taken the money out and was straightening it and putting it in order, turning it to face in the same direction, uncrinkling the corners.

As the train pulled out, he looked up and directly at Melanie for the first time. He just stared, and the window framed him like some bizarre portrait. As the train gathered speed, he moved from window to window, from frame to frame, and he kept his eyes on Melanie, like one of those trick pictures that seem to be looking at you no matter where you stand. The whole car had seen this. Now we wanted to eavesdrop on the explanation of Neil and his connection to Melanie. I assumed he was a former boyfriend—his situation was so much more pathetic when you thought that. And he was very young; how does one fall so far so fast?

But we got nothing out of her. We expected Arthur to comfort Melanie, but instead he sat with his chin lowered, gently shaking the quarters still held in his hand. His eyes stared at the floor; he was frowning.

We stared at him; we disapproved of him. We could see that Neil bothered him, that he wasn't prepared to deal with someone's *personal* beggar, and that neither he nor Melanie was going to mention Neil.

I am sure Arthur had a reason for this behavior. I don't know what the reason was.

For a week Arthur and Melanie took the same train, and they sat next to each other, but they rarely spoke. Then one day they sat with a seat's worth of space between them and someone took it at the next stop. From then on Melanie moved to my side of the car, and her face resumed an entirely neutral mask. I sympathized with her resignation. I had seen romance and disappointment and failure right before my eyes. Having only a few facts to go on never keeps anyone from drawing conclusions.

Take the clown, for instance: even though he was an unknown, a purely public performer, he was knowable. I'm sure he knew me as well. We never varied from the essentials, but occasionally I would get him by brushing a hand close to my jacket, as if reaching for money, or he would pretend to walk by without acknowledging me, only to stop at the very last moment. Every time I saw him he was angrier and he was losing customers. He knew this; up until the end he was able to stop himself by a supreme effort of will and do a tap dance or some ingratiating performance to garner the passengers' sympathies. But you could see the contempt in each gesture; you could hear the harshness in his voice.

The last time I saw him he had added an undersized fedora, held in place by an elastic band, to his costume. He was wearing makeup, too: a dramatic outlined teardrop at the comer of his left eye and cherry-red lipstick perfectly applied.

He came through the "Do Not" doors and stood watchfully, his eyes going up and down the car. I thought he was calculating contributions, and he wasn't very happy with the figure he came up with.

Finally, he honked his horn, over and over again. People glanced at him and frowned over their papers.

"Ladies and gentlemen, I'm collecting money for the homeless, for the helpless, for the people who don't have keys for any doors, people who once were just like you, the people you never want to see again. Ladies and gentlemen, reach in your pockets. What've you got? A nickel? What are you going to do with that nickel? Buy a house? Buy yourself dinner?

"Pinch your arms, ladies and gentlemen, your well-fed arms. Have you eaten today? There are people who haven't.

"What are you going to do with that nickel? Buy a coat? You've got two coats, you've got warm jackets, you've got shoes, you've got socks for all your shoes.

"What do you want then? A movie, a magazine, maybe a painting to put on your wall? Why not? You're not starving. Why not? It's *your* nickel. If people are dying in front of you, kick them away. It's *your* nickel."

He honked again. "Ladies and gentlemen, boys and girls. You don't need those nickels! You've got too much already." Here passengers straightened their papers in annoyance and slouched down in their seats. I knew their thoughts. If they had too much money they'd be in a limousine, or at least in a taxi.

"People are screaming, people are crying, and what do you care?" the clown continued. "If you can sleep easy, you're too rich! Where are the sores on your body, where is your stench? Are you keeping yourself alive with that nickel? Are you willing to kill for that nickel?"

"Oh, shut up," someone muttered, just loud enough for most people to hear, and there were a few snorts of agreement and a nod or two. The clown paused.

I don't know if he'd heard the rebellion or merely sensed impending defeat. His eyes blazed, but his cherry-red lips pulled back off his teeth in a pantomimed smile. "Ladies and gentlemen, lighten up. Tell me when I've pleased you," he yelled as he skipped down the train. "Tell me when I can stop." He got to the end of the car and spun around. "Did you hear the joke about the bag lady who lost all her fingers? No? She had to switch to a backpack!" His lips pulled tight again.

The train was going slower and slower. We were heading for Fourteenth Street now, and the clown held out his pail. "Ladies and gentlemen, boys and girls, a nickel, a dime, a dime or a nickel. Help the needy! End suffering! Do something important with your life! Anything you can spare, anything at all!"

He held his pail out, but too many people were disgusted with him or with the slow-moving train. He made his way up and down the rows and went back to the end of the car. I could see beyond him to the flickering lights of the tunnel behind us. He looked down at his pail and sneered.

"Fifty-six cents," he counted, and then he smacked his hand against the wall. "Fifty-six cents! Someone gave a penny! Who did that?" Suddenly he was furious, and he stomped down the middle of the train, lurching carelessly left and right. "Did you do that? Did you?" he shouted into various faces. One and all we denied it. "You think it's funny, do you? You think you're clever because all you can spare is a penny?"

We were bored or impatient; we refused to acknowledge him. I went back to my paper; most people stared out the darkened windows. One person asked another for the time. The clown irritated us by making us feel guilty.

Our studied indifference got to him. He began to honk his horn, and the noise took him over so that he forgot it, like a tic. He honked it whenever he paused, whenever he wanted to emphasize or threaten. It was incongruous and frightening.

He pulled on the emergency cord and the train screeched to a halt. Arthur jumped up as soon as he saw it and yelled at the clown. "Now you've done it!" he shouted. "You have no right to interfere like this, to take over!"

Melanie rose too. "Leave him alone, Arthur. I don't think you should get involved with him."

The clown, his lips peeled back in a cherry-red grin, strode to Arthur. "Are you the one? Did you put that penny in?"

"No. No, I didn't. I wish I had. You're a beggar. You have no right to complain."

"Can't be a chooser, eh?" the clown crooned. "I spend day after day here and all I ask for is mercy, but instead you want me to humiliate myself, to bend down, to shuffle. You won't give any money until I prove I'm not your equal."

"Oh, this is horrible," Melanie cried.

"I'm a person," the clown shouted. "I've got two hands, and I can hurt you with them!" He put down his pail and horn and raised both fists. It was peculiar how he held them in the air.

"He's a maniac!" a man yelled.

At that moment the conductor came through the doors. "Who pulled the cord?" Then he caught sight of the clown. "You again! That's it! Enough is enough!" He glared at the clown, whose fists were still raised in the air.

"Is there a cop on the train?" a passenger cried. "This guy is threatening people. I think he's crazy."

"Of course he's crazy," someone smirked. "Probably living on our money and never paying taxes. Do you pay taxes, clown?"

"There's no tax on a penny, is there? Is that what you gave? A penny for the poor?" He waved his fists.

"Look out! He's going to hit someone!"

I sat where I was, the newspaper in my lap. My face felt thoughtful; I'm sure I looked very thoughtful. The clown came over to me. "It was you, wasn't it? You put the penny in when I wasn't looking? It was you, wasn't it?"

He sounded pathetic. I gave him my disconnected squint, and someone said, "He's going to hurt that old man."

Arthur jumped forward and took the clown by the arm. "Leave him alone!" he said.

The clown backed off and moved to the end of the car. "Murderers!" he shouted. "You'll let someone *starve* for a penny!"

"He stopped the train yesterday, too," the conductor said.

"Throw him off! Teach him a lesson!"

"That's a little harsh," I said mildly.

The clown looked at me with contempt. He stood with his back against the rear door. His eyes traveled once again over the passengers in the car, and then he turned, unlocked the door, and vanished into the tunnel.

"Stop him!" the conductor cried, but we all crowded together to look out the door, ignoring the conductor. We were interested in the clown, now; we were looking for an anecdote. We saw him for the first ten yards or so, hopping down the tracks, but then he passed out of the train's light and into the dark

When he disappeared we began to move back to our seats, a little disappointed—not with ourselves, for the clown was so clearly insane we could not be responsible for him—but because we were cut off from the end of our story.

The group scattered, consulting watches. "You can't catch him now," a man told the conductor. "We might as well go."

The conductor wavered, mentioning regulations and snapping his flashlight off and on, but I think the complete willingness of everyone on board that car to be done with the clown (to move on is a natural and normal reaction) convinced the man that it was, indeed, proper to leave the clown on the tracks and go ahead.

Maybe he radioed someone in authority; I don't know. I got off at Fourteenth Street and stood on the platform, waiting for the next train to come in. I would be late for work again, but they didn't really care. They tolerated me when I came in punctually and when I didn't. I was the old gent, and I carried a newspaper and a fold-up umbrella, and I had an omelette for lunch two times a week. I could be late again, and no one would mutter.

Far down the tunnel a train blasted three whistles for a police call, over and over again.

I craned over the edge of the platform.

The clown was barely visible, emerging from the tunnel down the center of the track and heading toward the station. He was a dozen yards or so ahead of the engine, and I could see passengers crowded at the windows, heads and heads of them as the train crawled forward, squeaking its brakes, blasting its horn.

He led the train like a ruined Pied Piper; no, he was driven slowly forward by the train; it was like reality bullying a small idea.

Nevertheless, he elated the crowd on the platform, who at last could see the cause of their lateness, who could sense that this one would probably make the news. They were, all of them, quite pleased with the clown on the tracks, sooty and diminished. He looked odd, and he was silent; they could speculate at leisure.

The clown had lost his belligerent air, though he now had everyone's attention. I don't think he realized it. His triumphs had always been marked in small coins; he couldn't adjust.

Transit police jumped down and took him by the arm. More officers leaned over the platform and pulled him up.

Once he was in custody, the train gave three toots; not blasts, toots. I think the engineer was mocking him. The clown looked back over his shoulder, his eyes peering hard at the train, his fists starting to bunch. Strong arms pulled him away.

I did a little shuffle for him; the merest slide. He didn't see it. I doffed my hat, I raised my hand at his retreating back And then he was eclipsed by a wall of uniformed backs.

Our world was rid of him, well rid of him and his horn and the way he trumpeted his needs above ours. It's humility that's required, after all. Humility. Without it, there is no order. I know it; I look out for it; I myself am a humble man.

Lying There, So Quietly

He wasn't a beautiful man, in his coffin; it made him look too thin. It also, because of its mahogany or pseudo-mahogany scrollings, made him look uncomfortable. He belonged in a plain carved box.

Not that he hadn't admired ornate things; he had. His wife, her lips pursed painfully, her eyes uncertain but determined, had bought over wrought things, one by one, to fill up the house. They preferred simple things, simply fashioned, but they surrounded themselves uneasily with agonized cherubs on the mirror of the bureau, unhealthy grapes on the end tables, tortured maple leaves on the dining-room suite. It was all furniture that carried a conviction of taste—or so Rosalie thought, at least, as she considered her father. He was so strangely immobile, so far away, so frighteningly out of place in his own home. Everything she saw had a dreadful, grainy quality to it; after ten years she was home for her father's funeral and now home seemed like a copy of itself, done slightly the wrong scale.

And how had her mother, that worried little woman, managed to have the coffin at home, rather than at a funeral parlor where everyone, naturally, landed their loved ones? Rosalie turned her head slightly to the right to view her mother, dressed in distracted dark grays, her face wrinkled with crying and loneliness. Her mother—that poor, pathetic figure, looking somewhat shrunken now like Rosalie's father in the casket, the two of them smaller than they'd ever been before—was determined to act her tragedy out in familiar, heavy surroundings. And she was right to do it, Rosalie thought with a start and a rush of love: "Daddy belongs here."

For the first two days of the wake, Rosalie and her mother sat in the front row, on folding chairs supplied by neighbors, for an hour in the afternoon and an hour and a half at night. There were three rooms on the bottom floor of her parents' house: living room, dining room, and kitchen. Her mother could not bear to place him in the dining room (her eyes had narrowed to painful slits, her mouth had trembled), so they'd moved him into the living room (it haunted Rosalie every time she thought of it: my dead father in the living room), moved the sofas into the dining room, moved the dining-room table to the wall and the china closet out to the porch.

Rosalie's heart had jarred at every move of the furniture; it somehow made her father seem that much deader, but it had been done, with her mother's distracted directions, with the neighbors' help, with her uncle's help, with help, physical help—hands and faces emerging from the past. Her Uncle Matt had been there constantly, her mother's brother, large, red-faced, eager to do anything. "Just tell me what to do, Mabel," he said over and over to Rosalie's mother, and she blinked, pointed to something, and he did it.

It was amazing how big Uncle Matt was and how small Mabel was. "Well, it's a beer gut," Uncle Matt said, slapping his diaphragm, shifting in his chair. "Your mama never liked beer." But that didn't explain the difference in height, a good ten inches. "I took after my father, Mabel took after mama," he added matter-of-factly.

They were sitting at the kitchen table, the only table plain and square and unassuming, covered by red-checked oilcloth, salt and pepper shakers, and a plastic white napkin holder. Uncle Matt held the salt in his right hand, shaking it right side up so nothing spilled.

"Your grandma and grandpa (you probably don't remember them) were Mutt and Jeff, I guess you'd say. I outgrew mama by the time I was ten, never outgrew daddy at all. Evenest people I've ever known. They discussed things, you know, back and forth. How cool should the potatoes be stored? Should the dog have a bath in January? Keep the bedroom windows open or closed? They loved to talk. That's why Mabel loved your father, I think. We kind of got tired of listening to talk, Mabel and me. We could figure out what we wanted for dinner in two seconds flat, but our parents would discuss it for hours. Sometimes we'd have sandwiches while they debated; a roast or a stew, it could go on forever. I remember Mabel telling me your father was the quietest man she'd ever met, and what a relief *that* was. Well, I don't know, I like to talk myself, but it wasn't that your father didn't talk, really; it was just that he knew talking didn't take care of everything. He left a lot up to Mabel. Of course, he would. Mabel would rather just do a thing and take the eventual consequences than debate what the consequences would be. Well, you know of course why Mabel married your father." He settled back in his chair, his right hand hunkered over his bottle of beer, his brow slightly damp from the kitchen heat.

"No," Rosalie said, slightly surprised. She'd never thought about why her parents had married, they just *had*.

"It was summer. All the year long Mabel had been bringing boys home to dinner. She was nineteen and impatient. She brought them home, unannounced, like stray kittens, and left them in the kitchen with our parents. Well, your father, Alf, his shoulders were a little hunched, he kept his hands in his pockets, and he had this quizzical look on his face, as if he were slightly surprised. I didn't think much of him, he looked kind of *thin* to me, you know? Like you could move him easily if he got in the way. Well, I put out another plate. I always did that when Mabel brought someone home. It made it more fun, you see. It would always look like there would be dinner, and Mabel's date would always ask if he could help with anything. That was a sort of cue. Daddy would say, 'Well, thanks for the offer;' and tum to Mama and remark, 'Is there something he can do?' and she would say, 'Well, I could use some help peeling the potatoes if you want them mashed. Or do you want them baked?' And then they'd be off and running. 'Maybe scalloped, we haven't had scalloped in a long time: What about fried? With onion and paprika? That would be faster but nothing else is ready anyway, so time doesn't matter.' They could go on like that for hours. If they asked my opinion, I would always say, 'Anything's fine with me; I'm starving.' And of course Mabel was nowhere around."

Rosalie ran some water in the sink, rinsing out glasses. "Where was she?"

"In her room probably. She kept cheese and crackers in a bureau!" He went to the refrigerator and took out another beer, keeping the bottle cap in his hand, weighing it. "Well, Alf just disappeared. He never came back. Your mother had this twist to her mouth when she came down later and saw he'd gone. It wasn't the first time a boy had wandered away. I didn't think much of it at the time.

"And I don't mean your father just disappeared from the table. He disappeared altogether. He sent some flowers the next day with a note, 'Thanks for dinner;' and when Mabel tried to thank him, she found he'd left town. I think that impressed her. We didn't see him again for two years. And then one day he came back. Mabel was still at home, although I'd moved out. Got a job and relocated; ate most of my meals out, with no trouble picking something off the menu. If I couldn't make up my mind, I'd order everything that caught my fancy." He laughed and slapped his belly. "I guess it shows, but I like a simple life, I don't like confusion. Food's not the place to get stuck; it's not worth it."

Rosalie put on water for more coffee. "There's cake, Uncle Matt. Apple crumb." She put it on the table, and Uncle Matt reached for it.

"Don't mind if l do. Anyhow, Mabel liked the way Alf had just gotten up and left. Now here was a man who could make a decision. And it was convenient for her that he'd come back. So they got married, and a year later there you were. Of course our parents thought it all happened a little too fast, but they got used to it eventually."

Rosalie sponged off the counter and nodded. "I've heard parts of it. Where did Dad go before they got married?"

"Canada, he said. Said it was cold." Matt concentrated on his cake, and Rosalie poured his coffee.

"He said a raven fell into his lap, and that's when he knew he should come home," Rosalie said.

"That's about all he ever said about it, yes. But I never did believe that story. Out of a clear blue sky, huh? Suddenly tucked its wings in and took a nosedive. Never saw it happen."

"I always liked hearing it. When I was a child I would sit in the grass with my hands out."

"I think he read that story in a book."

Rosalie laughed in disbelief. "Why would he make it up?"

"Alf liked his myths. You don't think a man who would up and leave without a word, and then turn around and come back without blinking—you don't think that kind of man invents things?"

Rosalie thought of her father, that very small man, dull and comfortable as an old sweater. "I guess everyone dreams," she said thoughtfully. But it had never come up between them, this question of dreams. Her legs moved restlessly. Should she know what her father's dreams had been? She frowned, her eyebrows licking at her eyes. On Saturdays her father had worn a plaid flannel shirt and loose chinos and had walked around the house with a screwdriver or a paintbrush. Sometimes he had gone on the roof and cleaned the gutters. She had never thought there was more to it than that. He never said anything about Canada; she could not recall how she knew about the raven. Shouldn't he have told her more? Didn't he have a responsibility to tell her more?

If she wasn't careful, she would end up angry with him, for how little he had said, for how little he had left.

"Well," Matt was saying, finished with his coffee and cake, drumming his fingers on the empty beer bottle. Rosalie smiled uncertainly and looked out the window. "Weather's good," she said softly.

"It will hold for the funeral at least." Matt looked down at his broad hand, began to whistle, and stopped himself.

"I don't think I knew my father very well," she admitted.

"Oh," Matt said. "Well, children never do." He smiled shyly. "And I think he wanted it that way."

She nodded. "He never said anything but ordinary things."

"He liked ordinary things."

The next day was sunny, with a slight breeze. Rosalie woke up, vaguely aware of phones ringing and a rustle in the house, steps walking lightly in the hallway, voices lowered but urgent. She was in her old bedroom, and, though she woke early, she stayed in bed, alert. She felt embarrassed and odd, trapped between the remains of adolescent impatience and this newfound sense of having missed out on something important. She had gotten stuck on the day she'd first seen her parents as small and irritating, people who got in her way. Was she to blame for that? For having slighted them, for stopping there, for never looking back long enough to see if, perhaps, she'd discarded something important?

She shut her eyes and the voices still reached her. They were easy to identify, her mother's low and mournful statements, her uncle's lengthy and conciliatory replies. What now?

Her mother's back stiffened and Matt strummed his coffee cup when Rosalie finally joined them in the kitchen.

"There's your mother's good coffee," Matt said.

"She likes tea," Mabel said, turning on the burner under the kettle.

It seemed wrong to ask how everyone slept. Sleep well with a coffin in the house? Rosalie sat down, a determined smile on her face. She was careful to make the smile sad and ingratiating. She knew enough not to try to boil her own water or to take her own tea bag. She could tell by Mabel's back that her mother was in "possession"—determined not to sit or relax or unbend. It was impossible to pretend that something wasn't going on. Indignant whispers had been blowing through the halls for the last hour, and once again Rosalie felt like a child in a house filled with adults. There was something they knew; there were signals passing from Mabel to Matt and back again. "Yes." "No." "She's bound to find out!" "Let me handle it."

It irritated Rosalie, though she felt it was inappropriate, even bad, to feel irritated while her father lay just past the doorway and through the short hall.

"What is it?" she asked finally as her mother handed her a cup of tea. "Something's going on. You may as well tell me."

Mabel sat down then, her back turned slightly to her daughter, her hand resting on the table, facing the window above the sink.

Matt glanced at her, then back at Rosalie.

"We had a phone call."

Matt got up and poured himself another cup of coffee. Rosalie could tell he didn't even want it; he stood, staring at it, then sighed once and sat down again.

"There's something you don't know," he said with determination. "There's a woman," Mabel said, bitterness and triumph biting her words off short.

"When your father went to Canada," Matt said slowly, "he was involved with someone."

"A woman," Mabel repeated.

"And she's coming to the funeral," Matt ended sadly.

"She won't set foot in this house. This is my house."

"She's come to pay her respects, Mabel."

"She doesn't have any respect to give," Mabel said bitterly. "A woman like that."

"This must be almost thirty years ago," Rosalie said, surprised by her mother's rancor. "You resent his seeing a woman thirty years ago?"

Mabel's back remained rigid, her eyes cast out through the window. Matt watched her with a worried look.

"There must be more to it than that," Rosalie said slowly. "But I just can't see it."

Mabel turned her head to throw a chin-high, withering glance at her daughter. Rosalie was surprised to see the accusation in Mabel's eyes, the harsh, thin line of her lips. "You can't see it," Mabel said scornfully.

"The girl doesn't know anything; why blame her?" Matt said quickly, patting Mabel's hand and nodding sympathetically. Rosalie blinked hard. Why was her mother being comforted for being rude? Rosalie swore she wouldn't say another word; it was all beyond her. Maybe this was grief; how could she know? No one had ever died around her before.

"Rosalie," Matt said finally, still patting Mabel. He took the time to clear his throat. "The woman who's coming is your father's wife."

Rosalie paid no attention to the thin choked sound that came from her mother's throat. Her eyes stared straight at Matt, who looked deeply embarrassed.

No matter how surprising Matt's words were, they made immediate sense on at least one level. No wonder her mother was upset, she thought. Then an unpleasant idea hit her like a punch in the gut, that sudden.

"I am your daughter?" she asked Mabel, taking quick gulps of air.

"Fool," her mother snapped.

"Of course," Matt said, surprised. "Of course."

Rosalie twitched her shoulders. She could feel her cheeks burning. She thought she might be dizzy from the speed of it all, but she forced herself to think clearly-and bitterly. Her voice was cold. "I took it on faith. That I was, all these years. I understood it to be true. Just as I understood my parents were married. He was my father?"

Mabel groaned. "Slap the girl. Tell her nothing's changed."

"Nothing's changed?" Rosalie said sarcastically. She hated the woman sitting across from her. "My father wasn't married to my mother. Do you know what that makes me?" She felt a small bundle of self-righteousness grow, filling in the cavity where all her previous assumptions had been.

"Nothing's changed!" her mother repeated, turning to slap her open hand on the table. "Nothing's changed from ten minutes ago! I'm your mother, he's your father, and everything's exactly the same."

"The same!" Rosalie breathed. "The same as what? As what you knew or what I knew? How do I know about anything, anything at all?"

"You're upset," Matt said awkwardly, his big hand tapping her shoulder, his eyes darting over to watch Mabel. "Of course you're upset. It's a surprise, a shock. But don't overdo it."

"Overdo it," Rosalie repeated. "Why, I've just realized I have no idea what the truth is. You people could be anyone; I could be anyone."

"I've never raised a hand to you till now," her mother warned.

"Oh, God," Rosalie moaned. "Canada! Another wife! I might have family!" Her voice was astonished.

"You don't have family," Mabel snapped.

"How do you know?"

"Your family's here. We're your family."

Rosalie saw that her mother's eyes were moist and opaque, but she wouldn't allow herself to be taken in by any emotion other than her own; her own was big enough. "So you say," she retorted. "So you say."

But if she expected to keep her mother's attention, she was wrong. As if the sarcasm reassured her, Mabel turned to her own concerns.

"After all I've done," she said bitterly. "After all this time together, and that woman still thinks she has a claim on him." She shook her head, her eyes dropping briefly and then snapping shut. "It's too much for me. I'll kill that creature if she sets foot in this house!"

"Now, Mabel-"

Rosalie sighed. She gave in for a moment to her mother's will, as if she needed a rest. "I'm lost. What does she want?"

"She wants him back."

"Back?"

"She wants to take him to Canada and bury him there."

"Oh, God. What for?"

Mabel's mouth twisted. She adopted a mincing, grating tone. "'He's my husband. I'll get him in the end. He'll be buried where I want.' Proving a point. Getting back at me. Laughing at all that's sacred."

"It's a symbol," Matt agreed. "Certainly a symbol."

"Can she do it?"

"She says she has the papers. She says she can do anything she wants. Stealing him from his own home," Mabel sniffed.

"This is too much for me," Rosalie said, shaking her head. "Why didn't you and Dad get married?"

"He *was* married. To her. Matt told you."

"But why didn't they get divorced?"

"She refused to. The laws were stricter then. It was a matter of honor with your father to respect her wishes, no matter how it hurt everyone."

"It's a strange idea of honor."

"Your father was a very accurate man."

"Accurate," Rosalie echoed helplessly. The word sounded strange; it had nothing to do with the father she knew, and it was not the kind of word the mother she knew would use.

The phone rang, and Mabel's face stiffened. She glanced at Matt, who pushed himself out of the chair and lumbered into the hall for the phone. Mabel and Rosalie listened to the pieces of conversation, trying to imagine what was being said on the other end. They heard Matt mumbling, "Who said that?" and "Give me that number."

"Oh, Rosalie," Mabel whispered, small again and frightened, 'I'm afraid of that woman. She never lets go, she's death itself. I can't let her take him!' Her eyes squinted with tears, and, suddenly touched, Rosalie knelt beside her, stroking her arm.

"I'm sorry," she whispered, "but he's already gone, you know. You can't have him back now. What does it matter what she does?"

"We planned on being buried together," Mabel said stubbornly. "It all fits together that way." She stood up. "I'll make her see it. Besides, they must be Canadian papers she has. How can Canadian papers possibly matter?"

"Maybe she can do it," Rosalie said. "The law's the same in most places. Maybe you have to accept that."

Matt came back, tucking his shirt into his pants. "She's got a lawyer," he admitted. "They've done things to stop the funeral." He stood, watching them, straightening his clothes.

Mabel sat down, resting one arm on the table, almost perfectly straight out. "How can she take him from me? He chose me. She knows that."

"All these years I've been using *his* last name," Rosalie said suddenly. "Is it legal? Is that who I am?"

"Call the police!" Mabel ordered. "Call the consulate! They're foreigners, aren't they? Somebody has to know what to do." She stood up, as if she were going to take care of it immediately, then sat down abruptly. "We'll just lock the door. And not answer. What can they do to us? Break down the door?" Her mouth twisted wryly.

"You said 'they': You both said it," Rosalie pointed out alertly. "Who else? Who else? His wife and then who?" There was an eager quiver to her voice.

Matt grabbed her hand. "Remember whose side you're on, Rosalie. Remember whose family you belong to. Everyone goes a little insane when a parent dies; you lose part of your history. Just take it easy."

"I don't know my history," Rosalie laughed. "What's history anyway but what other people tell you? And how can you rely on that?"

"See how far you get without it," Mabel said sourly. "You get excited because the details aren't just so. What's a detail?" she sniffed. "It's not so important. The main picture counts. Intentions count. It had nothing to do with you; you weren't even around. It was private. We kept it private."

"Who else is coming?" Rosalie insisted. "Other wives? Or are there children? Are there a few more details here that got missed? Uncle Matt?" She looked at him brightly, but her heart was thumping as if she'd been running.

"No, don't bother," Mabel said to Matt. She turned to Rosalie. "That woman had a daughter."

"I have a sister?" Rosalie breathed.

"You can believe what you choose."

"A sister."

"She's just your father's wife's daughter. No relation to you."

"That sounds like some kind of funny puzzle."

Mabel stiffened. "Nothing funny about it."

"Oh, Mother—or whatever you are—give in."

"Oh, no," Mabel whispered, "I don't give in."

Rosalie frowned, and then she crossed her arms on her chest. Mabel cleared up the breakfast dishes, sniffing and muttering. Rosalie nodded to herself, studying the back of Mabel's head. She had never noticed how stubborn, how intractable her mother's neck was, how self-indulgent and secretive. How wrong.

Her mother finally turned to her and said, "Your father didn't want her; didn't want her or that woman. He wanted me. He wanted you."

"That's harsh," Rosalie said slowly. "He didn't want his own child? That doesn't sound like Dad. He was kind, I think. At least, he was never cruel."

"I don't care," Mabel said slowly, making each word distinct. "We're the only ones who mattered to him. He loved me." Her eyes blinked furiously. Her voice startled Rosalie; her mother sounded like a jilted lover, and it embarrassed her.

But even if Rosalie had to turn her eyes away, she could not escape the evidence that there had been passion there, that two of the most ordinary people she thought she'd known had committed themselves wildly, consciously, and passionately to each other, abandoned themselves, really. And she was their love child. It took the steam out of her, as if she knew all at once that she could never equal or surpass them.

She studied her mother carefully. She was still such a small woman. Decisive, Uncle Matt said. All right, Rosalie would allow her that decisiveness; she would not now start to think of her as an arrogant woman, a small, arrogant woman. Maybe it truly had been love that had kept Mabel and Alf together all those years. In fact, Rosalie thought bitterly, it probably was love—love of a kind she herself would never experience, because people no longer staked their all on love. Certainly no one in her own acquaintance would be capable of a deception so silent and strong. She had never seen it in her parents' faces, this obsession of theirs. Nor could she recall anything special, in all her years of growing up. Her parents had seemed normal. They had seldom even held hands.

Rosalie got up, leaving Mabel and Uncle Matt to their coffees and their murmurs of lawyers and wills. She went to the living room and sat next to her father quietly, counting over her revelations. She thought to herself, "I know who I am in this family—I'm the one who can be lied to."

Nothing showed in her father's face, no identifiable lines of passion or acquiescence. What kind of man had he been, after all? She didn't know that, just as she couldn't place the woman who was her mother. She was sure she could never know. She had manufactured her mother at different stages: when she was three, her mother had been comfort; at eight, she knew all the answers; when Rosalie hit adolescence her mother turned constrictive, and from then on settled into being narrow and old fashioned. She couldn't identify the woman now sitting at the kitchen table, a woman capable of passion, the kind of passion that made other people incidental.

Rosalie looked at her father again. His cheeks were fallen in; his bone structure showed so plainly. She had not learned to read the lines in his skin; each furrow was probably the result of some experience, like ground exposed to a long rain. She leaned closer and stared without blinking. When she kept at it, it seemed that he was breathing, that there was a subtle flutter just at the edges of his nose, like someone trying to hold in a laugh.

"I do believe I'm taller than you are," she whispered, and as soon as she said it she felt ashamed. She had said it to belittle him, to diminish him, because she already felt him turning into a myth. Or not quite a myth, that wasn't it, but a mystery she'd neglected. She could imagine someone beginning a story about Alf, then stopping to tell Rosalie, "You didn't know your father, but—" She'd known him all her life, and only at his death did she find out she'd known the wrong man. That was it, she thought, trying to pinpoint the problem. She'd known her father; she hadn't known Alf.

The bell rang, and Rosalie got up quickly and lifted the side of the curtains to peer out the window. Her eyes skipped at once to the younger of the two women, whose head was turned slightly away. "Does she look like me?" Rosalie wondered. Would she get any truth out of her, this sister, this fellow scavenger who also never knew her father, who had been bred on a different set of stories (the reverse side of the mirror, the other side of the coin)? What was her name? How tall did she stand? Was she curious, too, about Rosalie? Had she come with a blister on her heart?

Rosalie found herself inching toward the door, though her mother and Uncle Matt were so pointedly ignoring the insistent rings. "This is nothing like a betrayal," Rosalie thought. "I should have met them years ago; I have a right to meet my sister." But she had a sudden fear of their dark shapes and the sharp, insistent fingers that kept ringing the bell. Her father had left them, after all. What were they like? She could imagine their distrustful eyes turning to rest on her, the wicked stepsister, the girl who had all the goodies and still didn't have enough.

She stood near the door, listening to that terrible bell, to her mother's cries, to her uncle's embarrassed footsteps pacing the hall. Blood relations—so she had been told—stood without and within, wailing in their own outraged voices. She was struck dumb by their various keenings. She felt lost and alien and no longer recognizable, like the man she had called father, whom she actually believed was her father, cold and silent and forever removed from her, like a flower whose last petal dropped while she blinked.

"How could it all be done without me?" she wondered, and her grief cracked open. "How could it all be done?"

Notes From The Attic

PART I

I am a stoical woman. I do not fight when there is any kind of alternative to it. I prefer to think a problem through; sooner or later the solution becomes obvious.

I am a large woman. I was charming as a child, with that particular kind of solemn-eyed prettiness that always matures into plainness. In my adolescence I resented the loss of my beauty, but then I realized that there is a certain comfort to be found in plainness, and that men more often strayed with pretty women but stayed with plain ones.

I married when I felt that it was time for me to marry, after I had completed my studies in anthropology, sociology, and mathematics. It was a small, sensible wedding, and we moved into a modest apartment, and then eventually into a modest house in what was supposed to be an improving neighborhood. In fact, Jonathan and I have always been considered a typical couple, the kind hooted at by the very young and the supposedly political because of our placid indifference to the state of the world, to the state of our minds.

This makes me relish so very much more the fact that our lives are not what they seem; that behind my print dresses and Jonathan's fresh white shirts lies an architecture of deceit. We are what the tabloids long for: blank faces with a shocking secret. I have often imagined my picture in four-color ink spread on the rack at the local supermarket, how my neighbors would casually pick it up, leaf through it and replace it, hesitating only slightly, thrilled for the first time in their lives.

After all, honesty and uncompromising simplicity are slim virtues, and I am a large woman.

I always take things in stride, but I admire decisive personalities. My husband is one. He will consider a wide range of options—consider them quite thoroughly—and then decide unalterably. For example, when we first discussed marriage, we also discussed children. Jonathan said he wasn't interested in children. At the time it wasn't a pressing concern of mine, but over the years that changed. At first I smiled in pretended interest as my friends grew big bellies and considered layout sets. They moaned about their expanding waistlines; they were thinner in their ninth month than I was as a virgin.

I wanted a child for a variety of complex reasons. Paramount was an intellectual curiosity about what kind of issue I could produce. Second, fear of a lonely old age. Third, fear of regret.

Of course I knew that once the novelty wears off, a child often becomes boring, if not frequently irritating. Then, too, children do not fill one's old age; by that time, they are obsessed with their own lives. But very few people regret having had children. They may regret the immediate having of them, but down the road, for all save the mothers of ax murderers, lies satisfaction.

There is also a great deal to be said about the power that parenthood gives you. That power grows as the children do. Perhaps I exaggerate. Perhaps I have a vantage point in that I have led a convoluted life. But children, as they learn to talk, move, and decide for themselves, continually reinforce one's sense of superiority. After all, consider how long it takes them to learn how to tie their shoelaces. That one command, "Tie your shoelaces," repeated year after year, gives one an immediate and well-defined sense of authority. When you feel authority in small things, you move effortlessly to larger.

Perhaps that is why childless women seem to lack authenticity. It is not that they have denied their biological imperative or any other such male rubbish; they just have no one to boss around. They are still afraid of their mother's disapproval, afraid their husbands will leave them, or their bosses fire them—afraid, in fact, that everyone will desert them or yell that their shoelaces are undone.

I leave aside the fact that childless women tend to age slowly. They are children themselves, and that is their half of the bargain.

A man never has a child growing in his gut, and so has no real sense of wonder. But he feels that credit is due him, if for no other reason than that he has supposedly compromised his independence. My husband is right to insist on sterility. He is the kind of man who would lose too much of himself in his children. Would it be cruel, even wifely, of me to say that there is not all that much that can be sacrificed without strain? His error lay in thinking that his choice determined my choice.

When Jonathan was six, an uncle asked him what he wanted to be when he grew up. "Thirty," he said. "Thirty" to him meant freedom from restraint, from responsibility. It meant staying up late and sleeping late. It meant freedom from childhood. Should he ever decide to be thirty five, he might very well want children. But in his mind he is always thirty.

Our children show the same stubborn determination. They know there is some game to be found out. They have known it from the first. Ensconced in the attic with a nanny, a visiting mommy, and no daddy, they nevertheless draw their own conclusions.

Perhaps one of their nannies let something slip; I would not be surprised. One of them is sure to have told them tales of model families: daddies in homburgs, mommies in aprons. I foresaw this; it doesn't worry me. Let Lydia say, however innocently, "And what do you do when you're not here? Do you have a husband?" I do not blink.

I say, "How stupid of me! I forgot to tell you! I must be slipping! Didn't I tell you?" And then I leap into stories of what happened at the supermarket, made-up accounts of people and places, it doesn't matter what. They stare at me solemnly, teeth biting their lower lips, knowing that the truth will be put off again.

But why do I keep my children in the attic? Have I explained it properly? As I said, I wanted children, and so I approached Jonathan. It was one of those tender moments, Jonathan and I were nestled together in the darkness, and I said, "I've always liked the name Lydia." To which he replied, "Umm!" and I said, "For a child." He stiffened slightly. "I think you can put that out of your head," he said. "I don't want any children."

"It wouldn't be so bad," I answered halfheartedly. "We could find some one to take care of it, so that we both had free time. We could even fit up a room for live-in help, maybe a college student."

"I don't want a child." He curled his body up against the wall.

I know how this conversation seems, having repeated it to friends: the intolerant man, the anxious woman. But let's be fair: I knew all about it before we married. I liked the fact that he knew what he wanted.

"I want to ask a purely theoretical question," I said. "If you had to choose: I leave you or we have a child, which would it be?" He sighed wearily. "I don't want a child."

Now, the fact of the matter is that I do love Jonathan, and I could see we were at a deadlock. We each wanted separate things. One of us must necessarily, in the regular course of things, be disappointed. It was no fairer of me to insist on a child than it was for him to resist one. We both had rights.

But does life have to stay "in the regular course of things?"

Was there a way for him not to have children and for me to have children?

There was. There had to be. After all, a child is not a third arm or leg that cannot be hidden from view. What it would take was planning and determination, and perhaps a little luck.

The next two years I spent dedicated to my field, sociology. I worked hard and long. I took trips for business and for research, and Jonathan became accustomed to them. I published articles. I began to make a niche for myself.

The third year I became pregnant. I did not tell Jonathan. I was a large woman when we married and had gained more weight over the years. As my child grew I kept my shape the same. Three months before I was due I told my husband that I had a special field assignment for the next six months, that it was a rare opportunity and I wanted to take it if he had no strenuous objections.

He was unhappy; he would miss me; he realized what a chance this was. Couldn't he visit me, wherever it was? No, he would not object.

I took my books and papers and flew to a foreign land, where I planned to have my baby and write a book at the same time. There was no telephone, so Jonathan could not reach me. I wrote him letters, describing my life as I moved from tribe to tribe: Jonathan could not surprise me with a visit. When my time came I left the bush and was safely delivered of a daughter in the nearest hospital, in a foreign land. It was a strengthening experience.

I wrote my book, shook hands with my natives and, with a well researched address in hand, returned to Jonathan, dropping off Lydia with a full-time nurse who lived twenty minutes away from home.

My first week back with Jonathan was blissful. I felt content, accomplished, and thin. Then I rented an apartment, installed the nurse and the baby in half of it, and made the front hall into an office. I spent regular hours there, divided between research and my baby. I took regular business trips (not all of them business) and took Lydia with me.

I had two lives. I was a mother when I saw Lydia; I was childless when I saw Jonathan. Within both lives, however, I was becoming successful as a sociologist. I began to teach a lecture series at the college.

Lydia was two when I became pregnant again. I followed the same procedure: a long trip, a hospital, a baby, a book. That was Matthew. By the time I was thirty-five I had Margaret and three books. Our mutual friends thought of us as a very progressive couple; after all, so much of my time was free of Jonathan. I came and went.

I had close calls. Jonathan once surprised me in my office with two of the children, but I told him I was watching them for an associate. I felt exceptionally and eminently capable. But as the children became older, I wanted them nearer. Lydia could walk and talk, Matthew was being toilet trained, and Margaret was crawling. The bigger they grew, the more I desired to see them.

It was then I proposed to Jonathan that I convert the attic into an office. I had serious talks with him about privacy and sanctity of place, and how I would expect him to respect my isolation when I was up there; I told him I might even request that he never come up without my permission. He knew that I often worked late; I wanted to continue my profession without interruption, at the same time that I wanted to feel that he was closer to me, that we were joined together in the same house.

He was delighted. He dipped his hands into my hair, pleased at my obvious affection. I said I wanted, in fact, to convert the attic into a whole apartment, with an office, a bedroom, a bathroom, a kitchen. He frowned at bedroom. "Sometimes I take a nap at the office. It clears my head," I said.

"You could just walk downstairs."

"If we don't keep this completely clear-cut, then it won't work."

"I'm not home during the day," he said. "I wouldn't be here to bother you."

"A separate phone, a separate everything. It must be my own place, my office and my rest area. It's practical and logical. But, really, we must do it my way. My work is important."

Jonathan respects work. I used my money to remodel the attic. I had an emergency exit installed, in case of fire, or in case of Jonathan.

When it was done, I had a large office at the top of the stairs. I had spared no expense in materials and was reassured that the area was soundproof. Behind it lay the apartment where my children lived with their housekeeper. Her name was Betty, and she was the longest employed in a long series of sitters for the children.

May I digress for a moment about child care? I am a sociologist; I meet my people during interviews and research. I consider myself a good judge of character, and I do not mind hiring illegal aliens. It is easier, with them, to find someone willing to stay under cover for a salary. The added bonus is that my children have learned to speak foreign languages.

My sitters stay as long as they need to acquire whatever amount of money they have decided on; that is why I also inquire carefully about the size of their immediate family. The larger the family, the longer they stay. It was this kind of wisdom I longed to confide to Jonathan in the evening hours when we sat companionably, reading or chatting about the day's work. Sometimes, indeed, I felt estranged from him. He would catch me staring at him and smile, but I would be thinking, "That's Jonathan, that is the father of children who must remain unseen, this man who no longer knows me, who has never heard me sing to a baby, ripe and clean, clutched to my breast, whose imagination does not include Lydia, Matthew, or Margaret in any stage of their growth, and who, to be honest, frightens me sometimes because of his happiness despite all that I have concealed from him." And then I, too, would smile, and life would go on. Under the circumstances, I felt my children would never meet their father. They were large, happy children anyway; they observed the world with strong eyes and quick mouths. They were destined for unequivocal professions: architecture, building, research, nothing ephemeral like finance or horticulture.

In terms of the children hidden in the attic, all went smoothly for a long time. I felt secure. Of course I thought, sometimes, about exposure: what I would do, how it would turn out. I admit that I daydreamed that Jonathan would find the children, scoop them up in his arms, and say, "You've made a mistake! I've always wanted children. I'm the happiest man in the world!" Such situations are only possible in daydreams. God knows they would be silly enough in real life.

But it is impossible to guard against little mistakes being made, especially when children are involved. For example, when the children were old enough to find their way into the office overhead, to crawl, to knock things over, Jonathan heard noises. One day he said, as we sat reading our newspapers, "I think we have mice or squirrels in the attic."

I am not easily ruffled. I smiled and said, "Do you mean my interpreter, Betty? She's been working late recently."

He shook his head. "I don't think it's Betty."

"Then it must be the cat, dear."

"When did you get a cat?"

"Oh, a while ago. It was crying out in the back, poor thing. I keep her upstairs."

"A cat," he said musingly.

"A young one," I added. "Still plays a lot. That's probably what you heard."

"A cat, then," he said.

But talk of a cat, a clumsy interpreter ("There must be something on her mind; she's always knocking things over, and she goes into hysterics sometimes") can cover only so many mistakes. The children were getting too big to hide. It was impossible to stick a bottle or a breast in their mouths and have them fall asleep. I saw the inevitable coming.

Jonathan and I were finishing a cup of coffee after dinner. He had been quiet all evening. I could tell there was something on his mind. Finally he asked, "Have you ever read *Jane Eyre?*"

"Why, yes, that's by one of the Brontës, isn't **it**?"

"Do you remember the part where Jane hears screams in the night? She wants to know what causes them."

"Ah?" I said, interested. "I don't remember that part."

A meaningful pause followed. "I want to know what you're hiding in the attic."

My mind scrambled for an answer. Stupidly, vaguely, I repeated his question: "What I'm hiding in the attic?"

There is an interesting side effect to having secrets. You are, of course, in constant fear of being found out. And that fear is so specific that you forget how much more likely it is that an entirely different interpretation, based on someone else's fears, will be made.

Jonathan, it turned out—stolid and unyielding and with his shoulders hunched and his eyes, in fact, miserable—thought I was keeping a man in the attic.

"A man," I said, when I finally understood. "A *man?*"

"We haven't been very close lately, have we?" he asked weakly. "Maybe we both work too hard. Maybe—I don't know—maybe I don't pay enough attention to you. I've been thinking, lately, that we've been drawing apart. You're an attractive woman," his face turned scarlet, "and a successful one. I believe there are men who would love you."

I'm sure Jonathan found it hard to understand the sharp, large rings of laughter that burst from me. With me, however, laughter inevitably leads to tears. I am a large woman, after all, and the sheer expanse of my emotions tends to make them overlap.

Laughing, weeping, I fell into Jonathan's arms.

PART II

That evening (for whatever reason, and I have been considering reasons deeply) was a turning point in my life. It marked a division of thought, of feeling, of action. It is why, in fact, I am writing these notes. Everything from that night on ran together, without seam, like a good movie.

Like an actor in a movie, I can see Jonathan sitting there, even now, yearning to be comforted. I can see myself too, a large, dark figure struggling to comfort him. I told him there was no one else; even looking fitfully at other men drove me to despair. "They are not you, Jonathan!" I cried.

Clasped in Jonathan's arms (not an easy task for him, since I weigh more), we discussed our worries and our love. Finally I confessed to him that the noises he'd been hearing were nothing more than my interpreter, Betty, who stayed upstairs often when she was having domestic troubles; I was considering inviting her to stay permanently. Jonathan relaxed and finally said, "I've been thinking. You always wanted children, didn't you? It hasn't been fair of me, not entirely fair of me, to refuse. If you still want a child… Well, do you still want a child?" He was awkward; had he gone too far?

How wonderful is life. Because I have had three children secretly, be cause I have had to conceal them and therefore worried Jonathan, I am now given clearance to have a first child. I appreciate the irony, and I consider it. I consider also that Jonathan has been frightened of losing me, is relieved at retaining me: This is a dangerous time. What he says today in gratitude will be regretted tomorrow when he regains his sense of himself. I do not want children, I tell him, not at my age.

Can I explain the depression that assails me after this? I dislike Jonathan; Lydia stares at me with unfocused eyes; Margaret goes into a rage as her last baby teeth come in; I write papers that even I know cannot be published, that are disjointed and harsh.

What have I done?

Have I triumphed? Could I now, if I chose, introduce my children to their father? Would he accept them? Do I want him to?

After all, the children are mine, as much as the books I wrote are mine. I have created them, not only in the physical sense, but spiritually, conceptually. Their circumstances are unique and will remain so only as long as the attic remains their environment. Should they come downstairs, be folded into a normal family—well, then, where would their privilege be? And where would mine be? Together with Betty they remain a tribe I alone have discovered; they are my project, my research.

I know how cold this sounds. But even if Jonathan's wishes are genuine, even if he does want to have a child, how am I to present him with such a fait accompli? What man could accept it?

How am I (and this may be the greater problem) how am I to live with a man who finds he's been deceived to such an unusual extent? In fact, and I know it, the reason I am so dejected, so surly and unreasonable, is simply because he did not find me out. I moved my children to the attic and, logically, *expected* to be found out. Instead, I spend my energies lying to a man who will not, cannot, guess what I have done because it is beyond his imagination.

My disappointment has crept into my writing, too. Sociology relies on observation and deduction; it is disastrous to bring one's own judgments into play. And I find that somewhere, at some point, I have leaped to a conclusion, an explanation, that does not have enough supporting evidence. Actually, I know where these points occur: In my last book I even grew arrogant enough to include a whole chapter that was supported by mere hearsay. Yet no one challenged me. The reviews were congratulatory, the universities all put it in their curriculum.

Although perhaps, too, it didn't matter at all that I tampered with my evidence, distorted it. It's quite likely I was right, after all, whether or not I followed the formula.

What is the reason for my success? Why have I been able to do, all the way along the line, exactly what I've set out to do? Have I set my sights too low? Is it enough to have written three important books and created three secret children with no help from anyone? What other things could I have dared to do?

In fact, that is the key to my present dilemma. I find myself unable to talk to anyone with any degree of sincerity. That is what comes of having secrets. A successful secret, in a book or in an attic, removes one from ordinary society. Secrets inspire contempt for others.

And how far can I go with my secrets? I have told Jonathan that Betty and her children have moved into the attic. I even announced that I am moving there myself, with them, daring Jonathan to discover why. He has become even more concerned, more conciliatory. I tell him I need time alone and he ignores the fact that "alone" includes an interpreter and her three children, supposedly blue-eyed Mexicans. And he agrees to it, obstinately concerned for my good and determined to *be* good.

The children are gleeful at my presence, at first, until I shuttle them persistently to Betty. In shrill voices they demand to know when I will play with them. Where have I gone wrong? I am the twentieth century's version of the hero. I am what the magazine articles call a superwoman. In fact, if anyone knew the details of my career up to this point I would be on the magazine covers. I retract what I said earlier about appearing in the sensationalist press. The women's magazines, however, wouldn't touch me: I am too large. They would lose subscriptions if they praised me. And yet I think it important to be this large: I cannot be dismissed easily. I am not playing at being a little girl. I belong to the universe, not the designers; I continue the line of fertility goddesses, the squat figures of Cycladic art, as robust and powerful as the earth.

So my own move to the attic is not all that surprising. For a while I move around here uncertainly, and then I sigh with delight and settle in. It is here that I will come to terms with the world, alone.

Jonathan leaves notes under the door to the attic. They are love notes, articles about my research, questions about the household bills. Every few days or so he appears at the door himself, and Betty tells him I am still too busy to be disturbed.

It is like a courtship; I can imagine him standing there with wilted flowers in one hand. But I will not come down; I don't even peek through the keyhole. Nor am I, like the marriageable girls in certain tribes, keeping myself in a ritual hut until the male observes his share of the rituals. There are no rituals with the new superwoman—unless, of course, she invents them.

And am I inventing them? I am growing increasingly despondent about my life in this particular attic. Already I have contracted to build another addition, an attic on top of the attic, where I can be sure to escape the prying eyes of my children, Betty's concerned questions, the knock on the door, the telephone's determined ring. I have been here long enough now for my colleagues to wonder where I am, for my publishers to inquire about the next book. An enterprising graduate student has been writing me weekly about my reclusion. She is smart, that one; she has become sarcastic about my isolation. "Meditation," she calls it. And what am I meditating about? She is doing her thesis on my work, so she has to find out. Am I joining the great iconoclasts, she wonders, or has my inspiration petered out?

As I said, she's smart. That last question annoys me. It is hard being of the new order, the order of superwomen, because like any precursor, one must keep on doing. I cannot stop now, here in the attic above the attic where my secret children continue to grow, not quite abandoned by me, but consciously unclaimed and noisy about it. Betty says that Jonathan has taken to visiting the children; she allows him in more and more often. Jonathan, after all, now writes out her weekly paychecks, he questions her about the children and their father. Is he finally growing suspicious? Will he discover the truth in order to find me? And what if he does? Would I mind if he and the children shook hands and moved in together, with Betty still overseeing things, and me, rigid in the attic with my questions and my resentments, like the madwoman in *Jane Eyre* that started all this?

After all, I have determined my life. I have done it based on my own desires. If I desire, now, to spend the rest of my life encapsulated in one of a series of tottering attics built on top of each other above the house where my husband and the three secret children live—this, too, is a product of the new order I have created. Well, perhaps I have been unfair to everyone, the children, my readers, Jonathan (who, when I look closely, seems more and more to be the kind of decent man that our civilization has always desired to produce). Have I, then (and with me the new order of women), gone beyond the civilized man, the citizen, to find new boundaries in a new society? Am I doomed to my attic until other women seek me out—large women, dressed in horrid "thinning" stripes and the dangerous plaids of the oversized department—until together we come to terms with the new rules of the new order?

In fact, is there a new order, or am I merely a temporary sideline, a museum attraction, an interesting footnote?

Women have a tendency to look ahead, I have noticed. It is as true for "civilized" as for "primitive" societies. Even in the attic (which attic is it, I wonder, second or third?) I consider the future. I have been able to "do" everything, it seems. I have won my reputation and decided to lose it. I have had attic children and allowed them to move (as they have done now) down to the main floors, with their father, my husband. How he, the man I have loved and still love in a reminiscent fashion, has learned to deal with all this, no longer matters to me. I am curious (of course I am curious), but my "meditations" do not include him or them.

I am considering the evolution of the world, the society of the planet. That has always been my concern. To be frank, I have always interpreted it through my own experience.

Well, why not?

Even if I am alone in my attic, I have impact. Before me, down how many stairs, I have created a society. Sometimes I think of writing a book about that society, of going below to discover it and to research its basic beliefs. As a writer and a sociologist, I find people and I create people. As a woman I have done the same. If I go downstairs, I will once again be "doing." My very presence, every activity, will mean something to Jonathan, to Betty, the children, the graduate student who will not graduate until she finishes her paper, to the lost cats I may someday gather and store in my attics in response to their harrowed wailing.

Any move of mine will determine the new order of life; the first time I lift my hand will signal commitment. In this world, in this overcrowded technology that actually provides the perfect camouflage for revolution, all roads lie open, all sentences writhe waiting for their freedom, an unexpected fertility comes to pass.

I have buttressed these attics so they can support more. Each level recognizes another secret, another resolution.

I am growing greedy for another doorway; I can sense another secret beckoning to me, its movement quickening, its first nudge un-expectedly strong.

Simple Accommodations

Three months after Alice's life fell apart when Sam left her, she was lying in bed with only a light on in another room, staring at the ceiling. The TV was off, the radio was off, the stereo had been disconnected from its wiring, and she was just lying down, trying desperately to hold on to reality.

Silex and Velcro, her two cats, were behaving oddly. Neither one had wandered over to her, nestling under her arm or sitting on her stomach. Velcro, in fact, was mewing in a faintly worried way at the foot of the bed, on the floor. Silex was staring boldly at Velcro from the top of the dresser. "Here, Velcro," Alice said softly, clucking to the small orange cat still obstinately on the floor. "Here, sweetie." Velcro looked up at her, her tongue just sticking faintly out of her mouth. (Velcro was an odd cat; her tongue always hung out, and sometimes Alice would gently tuck it back in.)

But the cat didn't respond in her ordinary, wobbling way. Alice's thoughts fleetingly considered Velcro and how very uncatlike she was. Her stride was off, and she never moved gracefully. Her head bobbed; she always ended up with cat food on her nose. When she ran it was with a sticklike exuberance; trotting, maybe, was more like it.

But her thoughts drifted away from Velcro and back to the emptiness of the room. Or was the room really as empty as she had thought? Alice's eyes shifted back and forth from Silex's expectant vigil on the bureau to Velcro's persistent curiosity at the foot of the bed. Alice listened carefully; she supposed it was possible that there was a mouse in the room somewhere, or a large bug. But if so, the cats would be after it.

It was so easy to lie on the bed and ignore the possibility that something in the room was different. On the other hand, a certain alteration in the scheme had already shown itself, and Alice was duty-bound to investigate. "Nothing exists but the present day," she thought to herself, a litany that she repeated even though it offered neither comfort nor radical hope. But it enabled her to get up from the bed, turn on the overhead light, and look around her room. Having done so, she sighed and admitted to herself what the next step would be.

"I must be crazy," she said morosely, then got down on her knees and picked up the corner of the bedspread to peer underneath. She dropped it quickly.

"I am definitely crazy," she muttered to herself, and then, in a louder voice, said, "Get out from under my bed. I have a knife in my hand, and if you do anything silly, I'll scream as well." She waited for effect. Nothing happened.

Alice picked up the corner of the spread again. Definitely two feet. But no movement. The answer occurred to her immediately. Someone had placed a dead body under her bed. The reason—well, of course the reason was incomprehensible. But the fact remained.

She took a deep breath and moved up to the head of the bed, then lifted the spread again. She saw the side of a man's face, eyes open, staring up to the slats and springs of the underside of her bed. A dead man, certainly, she thought. And then the man's eyes blinked.

She dropped the spread again. Had her eyes played tricks on her? Was he really alive? If he was alive, then what accounted for his strange quietness even when discovered? Maybe she, in fact, had blinked. And, by some transference of sensation, had assumed it was the corpse? She had to take a closer look.

This time she considered the corpse for fully five minutes. Not only did the eyes open and close, but she could also see that the chest rose and fell. The corpse was alive. Perhaps drugged, and stashed under her bed for some obscure reason? Perhaps deathly ill and unable to respond? Paralyzed or bashed on the head?

She experimented. Tentatively she moved her hand up to the man's face. He closed his eyes. She pinched his hand, and he flinched. Alice bit her underlip thoughtfully, then went to the kitchen.

When she threw the pepper in his face he sneezed, covering his mouth and nose with his hand and then slowly turning his face toward her. He looked at her beseechingly; he said nothing. Alice thought she detected a single tear roll down from his left eye.

Alice replaced the cover and left him in peace. Should she call someone and say, "Excuse me, I have a problem—there's a man under my bed"? Who could she call with such a statement? A friend was out of the question— her friends had barely recovered from the round of tearful midnight calls after Sam left her. Friendships can take only so much.

The police? She could imagine having to explain the situation to them: "You see, it's not that he's a threat, apparently. He's not causing any trouble, so I don't have a complaint to file—although it's true I don't know how he even got there. But the main thing is that it's a very irregular kind of situation, you see. He won't say anything, and I don't want to endanger his life if he's hiding here out of desperation or something. On the other hand, maybe he simply lacks motivation, and at any rate I'm not at all sure how one is supposed to handle the situation tactfully. Shooting him would be out of line, under the circumstances, yet that's what I've been led to associate with finding a man under one's bed."

If she called the police, she would explain too much. She felt a strange sense of consideration or responsibility for that shadowy figure under her bed.

Alice dug through her kitchen drawer for the flashlight and shone it as delicately as she could on the man. He closed his eyes in pain and held his breath.

As far as Alice could tell (she felt rude and was therefore hasty in her survey), he was just an ordinary man with an ordinary face. Dark hair (the eyes were closed, so she couldn't tell their color), no "distinguishing features." His clothes were nondescript but not untidy. She could only assume he had not been under the bed for long.

Perhaps he was hungry or thirsty, though. Alice went back to the kitchen, frowning. She hadn't been eating much lately, and the refrigerator didn't have much to offer. She found a few crackers and a small piece of cheese. The milk was sour, so she settled for water. She placed the plate and the glass under the bed and went to the living room. She turned on the TV tactfully—after all, it was very likely that a man who chose to stay immobile under a bed would also have very discreet eating habits.

She watched all the news and part of a movie, thinking at the same time about what the sleeping arrangements should be. Finally, she got a set of sheets and a blanket from the closet and pulled out the convertible in the living room. The man was already settled into her room, after all.

She went back to the bedroom and said quietly, as if talking out loud, "I'm going to go to sleep now, in the other room. The bathroom is on the left just outside this room. The brown towel is clean, and you may use it. There's also an extra toothbrush in the medicine cabinet. I generally get up at eight and leave at a quarter to nine. So I'm just going to go to sleep now, in the other room. The orange cat is Velcro; the black cat is Silex. They are both very pleasant cats. Good night."

She turned off the light and left, taking her alarm clock with her. Velcro followed her in lopsided fashion. Silex maintained her vigil on the bureau. Alice, despite her best intentions, did not fall asleep quickly that night.

She was listening hard for sounds of any movement in her apartment.

All she could identify was the click of Velcro's too-long claws as she wandered abstractedly around the apartment, and the faint, soft thud due to her overjump as she finally found out where Alice was sleeping. Velcro sat next to Alice's face, her head drooping slowly down till her slightly protruding tongue touched Alice's cheek. "Velcro, pull your tongue in," Alice whispered, and then she picked the cat up and arranged her in a comfortable position. Sometimes poor Velcro forgot that sleep required a different posture. And the sad part was that she seemed to be aware of this forgetfulness, spending long stretches of time with unsuccessfully thoughtful stares.

Alice never heard the man move. The silences were all familiar silences, despite the fact that there was an extra set of lungs not far away, taking in air and expelling it. Maybe this was what confused Velcro even more than usual.

In the morning Alice moved quietly, closing the bathroom door with a gentle click. She did not, after all, know the man's sleeping habits.

She thought she detected that his towel had been used, but if so it had been very neatly refolded. She left the bathroom spotlessly clean.

She set out a cup and put water in the pot. He could choose to have black tea or coffee, if he wished.

Alice picked up all the morning newspapers on the way to work. She scanned the headlines quickly when she got to her desk but saved the bulk of the search for her lunch break. At least there was no maniac on the loose that fit his description.

Ever since Sam had left Alice, the women in her office had made special efforts to "support poor Alice in her hour of need." There had been many lunches, after-work drinks, invitations for "heart-to-heart" talks and dinners, until finally Alice had gotten sick of the whole business. She no longer wanted to talk about Sam to anyone. Sam was not the same kind of lover who had deserted women everywhere; Sam was special, himself, not to be lumped with those other men about whom women huskily said, "I know exactly what you're going through. I was devastated when—"

So at some point Alice had refused to talk any further and set her mouth in a tight half-grin and got through the day without mentioning Sam.

But the day after she'd found a man under her bed, she suddenly began to ask very vague questions—suggestions, circumlocutions, hesitations, and downright evasions—about how one can go about seeking help for someone possibly catatonic, perhaps desperately avoiding confronting problems, in short, an individual in some sort of personal trouble.

Her coworkers looked across at each other. One raised an eyebrow; the other pursed her lips in a silent whistle. One assumed Alice was talking about herself; the other decided Alice had replaced Sam with an even more damaged personality.

In either case, they had nothing to offer but the names of their own therapists.

Alice called her apartment once, during the day. It occurred to her that the man might be lonely. She hung up after six rings, certainly enough time for him to roll out from under the bed and pick up the phone on the nightstand, if he so chose.

On the other hand, he might have left as inconspicuously and noncommittally as he'd come. The thought depressed her.

She went straight home from work and immediately checked under the bed. He was still there. She went out again and bought a load of groceries, racking her head to think of suitable things to eat in a reclining position. Soup, for example, was out of the question. She settled for sandwiches and fruit and (a final thought on the way back home) candy bars.

She fixed two separate plates, his for under the bed, hers for the kitchen table. She went through the personal notices in the papers; no one reported a missing person at all like the one she now had. For amusement, she considered placing a "person found" notice in the lost-and-found section. Perhaps someone would step forward with a suitable reward, undying gratitude, and a reasonable explanation.

What was the man's name? Where did he come from? How long would he stay? Where would he go next? Would he ever speak to her? Come to think of it, she hadn't said much to encourage him, either.

So Alice went back to the bedroom, cleared her throat and said, "By the way, my name is Alice, and I'm not angry about your being under my bed. It is a little unusual," she said uncertainly, "but that's probably only because I don't know the circumstances leading up to it. If, at any time, you'd like to talk to anyone about it, I'm always willing to listen." She stopped, trying to think of suitably encouraging yet reassuring things to say. "I can be very understanding and sympathetic. And I wouldn't pry."

There was, she thought, an almost detectable half-cough or tentative clearing of the throat from under the bed. She was encouraged to believe this was an acknowledgement, a sign from the man that her offer was appreciated and noted.

It did not take her long to fall into a routine including the man under the bed. She brought him food and removed his plates. She went so far as to buy him a set of clothes so that he could wash and change (he did this while she was out; she made a point of announcing her scheduled arrivals and departures). She went into the bedroom every day and spoke to him. She described the weather, what was happening in the news, incidents at work, anything that occurred to her.

She even told him about Sam, about the great wound in her heart. "Do you remember the fairy tale about the loyal servant to the king who wore three steel bands around his chest to keep his heart from breaking at the king's misfortunes? I had those bands across my chest, you see, and two of them have broken clean through, and the third I think is seriously cracked. I can feel it shudder sometimes and sense that it's about to go too. Is that what it's like for you? Is that why you live this way? I wish you'd tell me, because I'm becoming concerned about you. Do you think this is really the right thing to be doing? Are you accomplishing anything? And what do you think about, all day long, just staring at the slats? You should get some exercise. God knows everyone keeps telling me to exercise, that I'll feel better, and at least I don't stay on my back all day."

But conversations like these never got her very far. The most she ever heard from him was a sigh, and it was hard to tell whether that was from sympathy, boredom, or despair.

So Alice continued on this way for three weeks until one night when she felt she could no longer endure the silence from under the bed.

It had been a bad day altogether at work. There were rumors about layoffs, and Alice had suddenly realized she had the least seniority. She saw this thought mirrored in the bright, safe eyes of her coworkers. One of them even said, "Thank God it won't be me. My husband is out of work; I have responsibilities. I hope they pick people who are alone and free."

Alice turned to say something but stopped. She suddenly saw herself through their eyes—worried, dull, capable of surviving on less.

She thought, "It's not true. I've always wanted more, not less." She pictured the stranger at home; "I do have someone," she thought. And, for the first time, she resented the man's bizarre behavior, how he refused to talk to her, how he thought only of his own sorrow and never of hers. She didn't even know his name; he couldn't make the effort. She couldn't refer to him or mention him, because if anyone knew they would think her insane, and, to be honest, she deserved something, she deserved some sympathy, some kindness. She felt pushed to the breaking point from lack of kindness.

She rushed home from work and ran into her bedroom, not even bothering to take off her coat. Silex was back on the bureau, Velcro drooped at the foot of the bed. These were now their usual spots. Alice's heart was beating fast. She said, "I feel so terribly low. I don't know what to do with myself. Can't you please, just this once, come out and talk to me?" She started to cry. "You must know what I mean; I want to hear another voice. You stay there all the time, and I talk to you, I do what I can. Can't you talk to me? It would mean so much, just this once." And she stood there, with the tears streaming down her face and Velcro mewing at her with concern, but there wasn't a rustle or even a sigh from under the bed, so Alice scooped up Velcro and ran into the living room, her heart howling, the last steel band on her chest desperately unstrung.

She paced the floor with Velcro clinging onto her shoulders, her claws dug in deep. "I don't think I can stand this," she whispered to her cat.

She wanted the man to acknowledge her. She needed, right then, at that very moment, someone to recognize her existence.

She stood still in the middle of the floor and yelled for help, at the top of her lungs, over and over again. Surely even a man who lived under a bed would come out and rescue her? Certainly he would hear her fear and terror and despair and crawl out, if he had to, to offer what aid he could?

Suddenly there were fierce poundings on her apartment door, sounds of neighbors' voices, voices that stated, "What's going on in there? Open up! Open up!"

That was more than Alice had expected—much more than she wanted. Still clutching Velcro to her shoulder she called out weakly, "I'm coming," and opened the door.

There were all the people on her floor, craning their necks, passing comments, looking past her into her apartment. Some of them carried things—books, lamps, a flashlight—and one even brought a dog.

They pushed past her and stood in the middle of the room.

"I'm sorry," Alice said. "I'm so sorry. I didn't realize…" she broke off.

They wanted to know what the matter was, of course. Alice could see it coming.

She began to laugh, out of nerves at first and then out of the simplest, purest sense of irony. She knew he would be gone by now; she should have considered that. But it was obvious what she was going to have to say, it was mocking her even as she thought of it. And so, as everyone stared and Alice laughed shrilly, almost hysterical (someone was bound to claim that), she finally said it.

"I thought there was a man under my bed."

The Broadcast Storm

Bria blinked. No, it was true. There on her terminal, words and sentences marched from the left and slammed into words and sentences marching from the right. They tumbled down the center of her screen like they were falling down a well.

"God, no—data collision!" she murmured, alone in her office. Both her phones rang, and she asked the first to hold as pleasantly as she could and picked up the second line. Her fingers flew over her keyboard, pounding her ESCAPE key with determination.

"Bria here."

"My article, Bria," the managing editor yelled. "Where the hell is it? I had it on my screen, and the damn thing *scrambled!*"

Three people appeared in Bria's doorway, waving their arms at her. "We're having system problems, sir," she said firmly. She was the technical driver for the computer system that the whole company used. People got nervy around computers; she had to calm them down and baby them through problems with their individual computers or with the Server, the computer that controlled the network lacing them all together.

"Get it back!" he yelled and slammed the phone down. The line lit up again immediately.

Three voices hit her from the doorway: "I can't get my file." "Everything I did is gone." "I've got a report due, Bria!"

Bria spun her chair around, stretched her smile open, and said, "Just a temporary glitch. Give me half an hour to work it out."

A new voice behind them cried, "There's a bunch of words on my screen, and none of them are *mine!*"

Bria thought, "Chatter burst," and her heart sank

"Why don't you all take an early lunch or something? I'll have to adjust the Server, and that can take a while." Bria kept her voice pleasant and unalarmed, the way she'd been trained to at the academy. Never show fear. She casually tried to turn off the computer, but the switch did nothing. Marching and opposing lines of data continued to collide across her screen; the Server was in control.

"Bria," her friend Fontayne whispered behind her. "There's something very strange happening on the other side of the building."

Bria groaned. Her side was business, archiving, systems, and communications for *Alchemy Today,* a magazine devoted to metaphysics with a New Age slant; it included recipes. The other side of the floor housed secretaries, writers, and the various grades of editors. A lot of them had nasty tempers, and all of them had pull.

Fontayne paused outside the office of the letters editor. They had heard a pleasant hum as soon as they turned into the corridor; once they looked through the doorway, they saw the editor bathed in a blue glow from the screen-saver pattern on his terminal. The screen showed a gently ticking metronome that swayed in time to a melodic and soothing piping coming from the computer. The editor had a stupid, relaxed grin on his face. He was immobile.

"Subliminal hypnosis," Bria said. "His screen is locked into autologic."

"What's that?"

"Automatic animated logic. It's a monitoring device to make sure that the computer's devices stay in line. It thinks the editor is a printer or some other kind of machine."

Fontayne snorted; she had once known the editor in a carnal sort of way and thought about him pretty much as the computer did. "Well, can't we disconnect him somehow?"

"It's dangerous to break this kind of link; they're symbiotic now."

"Still, it might frighten the others:'

"Let's shut his door," Bria suggested on the way out. "That hum in there—it's better if no one hears it." She walked down the corridor quickly, wondering how extensive the computer corruption was. They came to the corral of proofreaders, where they heard anguished voices. Dempster, the copy chief, came running up to Bria. "It's the commas," he cried. "They're all in the wrong place. We keep moving them, but they move right back."

"Look, Dempster, we've got Server problems; it's serious, and it might take a while to fix. Can't you just leave the commas where they are? I'm sure no one will notice."

He shook his fist, spit in her eye, and turned away.

"I've never seen anyone actually spit on a person before."

"I don't think he really spit, Fontayne. I think it was a power surge of some kind."

"It was spit," Fontayne assured her. "And someone else is yelling down the hall."

As they passed one office, a man popped his head out. "Every time I try to dial out, I get switched into one of those dating lines."

Bria involuntarily flinched. "The phones! I should have guessed. It's our communications links to the network. The Server's taken the phone lines."

"I don't want a dating line."

"I wonder how far it's spread. Just this floor? The building? The city?"

"Listen, I've *already tried* dating lines. I mean, for an article."

"I'm beginning to see a trend here," Fontayne said. "It seems to me there might be a plan to all this."

"Don't be fooled," Bria warned. "That's just the programming architecture. Computers spend all their time evaluating; it's all this 'if yes, then do A; if no, then do B' stuff. Computers are always sorting, and after a while people suspect they're thinking. But they're not. It's called artificial significance."

The next office on their route belonged to the music writer, and Bria noted a flicking, unsteady light projecting out to the hallway. When she looked in, she saw the writer chasing letters of the alphabet that were simply cascading off his screen and falling on the floor. The writer kept trying to scoop them up and press them back onto the screen. He had a very determined look on his face.

"A textbook case of escaped characters," Bria marveled. The two women watched for a moment and then moved on.

"Did you notice that he's chasing letters and the letters editor is listening to music?" Fontayne asked timidly.

"Crossed files," Bria answered. "Every possible computer glitch is acting up. All the weaknesses, all the possibilities." Her voice was hushed. "There may be greatness here."

Fontayne halted. "Do you think someone actually made a *change?*" They were, after all, *Alchemy Today;* every year there was an article about a rumored transformation: hair cream that was really wrinkle cream, fruit molds that could fix the ozone layer, electromagnetic rays that cured cancer.

"No," Bria answered. "Well, not a true change. It's been discussed as a possibility in programming circles." She stopped and tilted her head thoughtfully. "A pyramidal cataract. If this is one—and everything we're seeing points to it—" She closed her eyes briefly and rested against the wall. "It could make my career."

"What's a pyramidal cataract?"

"Well, you know, every program is just a set of instructions. Every computer here has, say, twenty or thirty programs running at any time. Plus they're all connected to the Server, which has another thirty programs running, programs that control the activity of everything it sees. Well, there are routines in the Server that just check for errors, but the errors have to be listed so they can be identified. If the Server encounters a situation it hasn't been taught to recognize, it just can't see it." Bria drew in her breath. "A pyramidal cataract occurs when programs combine in error, but the new combination makes logical sense. It's like a room full of monkeys writing Hamlet: it's a theoretical possibility. Well, it happens to the programs; they keep combining to form a new program, which combines with another, and the new one still obeys the laws of logic until there's only one program left—the top of the pyramid—and all the machines are locked under its control. The program is so complex and extensive that the whole network processes all the instructions compulsively. In theory, it overheats and eventually burns out in a blast of magnetic energy called terminal discharge. But no one's seen it. It's high-level theory." She looked down the corridor appreciatively, noting its pulsing doorways and distracted, shouting inhabitants.

"Bria," Fontayne said softly, "that could be dangerous."

Bria winced, but even her wince turned into a completely blank expression when she saw the figure of the managing editor heading toward her. He was a small, old, mad man whose temper was so visible it suggested steaming pots and vats of vengeful potions. This kind of image sprang to mind, despite the magazine's professed allegiance to modern science.

"You! Bria!" he pointed as he strode along.

Bria stiffened. "Don't drop your eyes," she reminded herself. "Never lose eye contact."

"Dammit, girl, this is costing us money! Why the hell can't you get the damn thing working?"

"We have a serious network problem," she said neutrally.

"It's your job to *keep it running*," he barked. "You can't do it, out you go. I'll give you fifteen more minutes, and then we'll buy some typewriters. Get it?"

"Got it, sir," she answered pleasantly. "And fifteen minutes it is." He turned and stomped back to his office.

Bria turned to Fontayne; her smile was fixed, and her eyes had a hectic sheen to them. "You're right, of course. There's no real choice. Lives could be at stake. I have to stop it."

Fontayne was astonished. "You know what to do? But I thought you said this was an entirely theoretical problem. How could you know how to fix it?"

"There's always the deus ex machina—the god in the machine."

Fontayne looked puzzled.

"It's a literary thing. You know, in the Greek plays a god always descended at the end and made everything all right."

"What god can you get?"

They were back at Bria's office now. She pulled out a small black box she kept under the sofa and sighed. "This will cost me everything. Everything."

"What is it, Bria?" Fontayne trailed Bria as she headed out of her office and down the west corridor, toward the Server.

The whole corridor was blinking. Through open doorways they saw people arguing with their screens, jamming on their keys and shaking their fists. In one office a sharp light like a beacon stretched out from the screen and began a methodical sweep for the financial officer who was hidden behind a curtain. One secretary complained that she heard the sound of coins falling every time she sat down, but there was never any change on the floor. Her screen winked. One very shy man, an auditor, sat with his hands folded and a delighted look on his face, as the screen whispered, "You are perfect. You are perfect."

"If only I had more time," Bria moaned. "Fontayne, remember every thing you see. Memorize it, write it down as soon as it's gone. Oh, they'll never believe me! But you're right; it's too dangerous to let it go on."

The Server occupied a large corner office; when they opened the door they saw the room bathed in a violet light. A mellow, busy humming came from the Server itself, which was surrounded by tape drives, printers, and monitors. The tune seemed to be "Oh Happy Day."

"I just wish I knew how it all happened." Bria clutched her black box and approached the Server. Its screen showed fields of flowers swaying in the wind. The flowers sprouted feet and marched into factories where, still singing, they assembled more and more computers. Waves of the song swelled up and then switched to a single happy voice as the workers changed back to flowers.

"What's this all over the Server's keyboard?" Bria asked angrily.

Fontayne picked up a plastic bottle that was on the floor. "Something's spilled," she said and read the label. "Why, it's a sample of something called "Organic High Flush.""

Bria grabbed it out of her hand. "It's fused some keys and shorted others. What is this stuff?" She squinted. "A laxative! It's a freak of some kind—a supercolonic collider! That's got to be it! A one-in-a-million accident!"

"We'll keep it as evidence," Fontayne promised.

Bria's hand tightened on the black box as the ranks of flowers burst into the chorus of "Oh Happy Day." Her eyes were hypnotized by the marching factory workers. For all she knew, this could be how whole new worlds evolved. She shook herself and opened the box.

"What is it?" Fontayne whispered.

"A magnet. It will wipe out all the memory on all the disks. The Server will be blank." Gritting her teeth, Bria clutched the magnet and passed it around the Server's hard drive three times until the screen went dead on the last drawn-out chord of "Day."

Down the corridor they could hear a sudden silence and then, while Bria packed her magnet back into the box, a growing roar as people ran into the hall and screamed, "Where's my file? Where's my file?"

Fontayne turned inquiringly to Bria.

"That's right. All their files are gone. I had no choice really."

"Gone? He'll fire you!"

Bria snapped the black box shut. "I suppose I'll have to comfort myself with having the moral advantage. For all we know, the place could have gone up in flames. Overloaded circuits everywhere we turned. It's worth a few files, isn't it?"

"Ah, Bria, I'm sorry."

But Bria was already beyond her sympathy. She looked at the people cursing her as people she had saved; the offices she passed were like the bedrooms of rescued children; she heard the bell of the elevator beckoning to her like the wake-up beep of her own familiar screen. When she walked into the sun the world seemed safer and freer, and—to safeguard that freedom any way she could—Bria pulled the head off every flower she passed.

The Second Coming

On the morning of her thirtieth birthday, Jan sipped her juice with a delicate air, ignoring the two flies circling the table. "I am here as your God," she said.

Her father, Michael, looked at her once with a guarded eye, then shifted his gaze to Jan's mother. Ellen was a woman who preferred to believe what she was told. She would like to believe that her daughter was God, that "God" was used, perhaps, in a new way she was unfamiliar with—but Jan was too delicate to be convincing, no matter what kind of god she meant. She was small and refined; she had a tiny pointed chin and a sprinkle of freckles like a flush across her nose and fine hair that never kept its shape. She nibbled at food: spare mouse-like intrusions, little hummingbird sips.

Ellen was aware that spirituality was popular again, but her daughter had never been trendy. She was always distinctly separate from her mates (not friends; Ellen had long ago given up the hope that Jan would have friends). As a child Jan had stood and stared out the window, at other children, or up at the sky. She had smiled with good intentions when sent outside to play, but she could be taken over by absorption, have it fall on her like a hood. Ellen had, more than once, gone out to find Jan where she'd left her hours before, standing stock-still, her eyes squinting at clouds. Sometimes the child had even wet herself, she was so supremely concentrated.

The adult Jan projected utter calm, an immaculate peacefulness. She lived with her parents in Queens, taught school as a substitute teacher, rarely had a second date and never a third. Ellen suspected that her daughter was a virgin, and, what's more, would always be a virgin, out of sheer indifference.

"It's time," Jan said, rising to collect her books and her small token sandwich. Michael shook his paper and pushed his coffee cup back and forth. It was decaffeinated coffee anyway; he resented it, but, after his heart attack the year before, he was secretly grateful to be permitted anything.

After the door closed, Michael said, "I wouldn't even let a *son* of mine be God," and snorted, pleased with his irony.

Ellen shook her head; in her heart she wondered if there would be a miracle of some sort, because she didn't know if she could believe Jan otherwise. Two flies landed and inched toward the sugar. Ellen glanced out the window and saw that it was a fine day.

Since the time had arrived, Jan headed not for school but for a house in New Jersey that had, for the past three months, been visited by the Virgin Mary.

The Virgin descended from a grotto built in the backyard, touched the ground, glided forward, and then spun around before leaving. She was dressed in a blue mantle over a white dress with sandals on her feet, which seemed dusty even in the rain. A statue dressed in the identical blue and white stared at her from the grotto, but she seemed unaware of it.

Some thought that the peculiar swirl indicated preparation for the ascent into Heaven; others thought, but didn't dare to say, that she danced.

The Virgin came on alternate Wednesdays, and the cars and people who came to look stretched for miles. They came with petitions, cameras, notebooks, rosary beads, and folding chairs. The neighbors complained, the police complained, the mayor complained, but the Virgin still came on her own schedule, silent and twirling her skirts over dusty feet.

The household that the Virgin visited had a mother, a father, and a teenage daughter. They were the Simonsons.

Jan parked her car a mile away and walked to the house past the honking, snaking line of traffic. The crowd increased for the last few blocks, but Jan insinuated herself through the people (most of them very large people) until she came to the back of the house, where rows of men and women sat in folding chairs facing the grotto, with one eye on their watches. The Virgin was due at noon.

At 12:00 exactly the sun broke through the clouds, the Virgin descended from the grotto, stepped forward to the spot where numerous petitions for mercy had been placed, and swirled.

She was about to step back again when a small voice said, "Over here now, please. It's time."

The Virgin's eyes lit up, and she held her skirts high with one hand as she stepped out of the pile of pleas and moved swiftly forward. "These visitations, Jan," she said sweetly. "So very rigid."

"It's what they wanted, unfortunately."

The faithful rose up around them, some of them weeping and a large number of them appalled. "I knew it was a trick all along," a voice said firmly.

"Now that she's close-up I can see it's not her at all," a woman cried. But others, of course, closed their eyes and fell to their knees.

"We'll have to hurry," Jan said, "while they're still surprised. We want no bloodshed here." Her voice had a prim, teacherly quality to it.

"They like a show," Mary said neutrally.

Many of the cars were still trying to get to the house, although they were late. Some looked worried at the sight of a hurrying Madonna, but they all continued on. Jan, who was familiar with the route, crossed to the emptier side of the street. The Madonna was the first to hear the sounds of someone calling behind them, and she turned, putting a hand on Jan's arm to slow her down.

"Take me with you!" a woman's voice pleaded.

"It's Mrs. Simonson," the Virgin said. "She stared at me from the kitchen window while her husband had his picture taken. He's a man who keeps his eye on the story. She merely waits." They stopped until Mrs. Simonson caught her breath, and then Mary and Jan turned to push their way through the crowds. Mrs. S. followed.

They broke through suddenly, and Mary observed, "You know, the ones who didn't see it will doubt it, and the ones who saw it will disagree."

Jan sighed. "It's always the same problem. Which is the true message: the one I give, or the one they receive?"

"That's one of those false questions," Mary said. "The truth can't depend on the listener's understanding."

"All truth must be intelligible."

"Interpretations are what kills the truth. No one lets it stand alone, undefended. You say, 'Do not kill;' and they say, 'Kill what? Kill when? Kill how?'"

"Excuse me." Mrs. Simonson, a stout housewife with permed gray hair, put her hand on the Virgin's arm. "I've been looking out that window at you, looking and wondering. My husband kept saying that you chose *him*, and I thought, maybe not. I thought maybe you were making a point of *not* choosing him, because you never even looked at him, not once. Miracles are like that; they're never personal, are they? A miracle is like an accident, and if the same accident keeps happening all the time, then somebody's making a point, aren't they? You're saying the same things keep happening, over and over. It has nothing to do with my husband. I wanted to tell him that. I wanted to say, What? Does she have a watch?'"

Mary smiled. "I was about to change to daylight saving time. It would have amused me just to stay for that."

Jan said, "Exactly. That's perceived truth. It's what I was talking about: Time doesn't change just because the clocks are changed."

"There is no time without clocks."

"In our house, all the clocks are five minutes fast."

"It's the idea that matters most, you see. Almost no one's clock runs on time." The Virgin nodded her head, her fabrics flying.

"They all agree to let someone else be responsible for the time. What they don't realize is that when they change the clocks, they change midnight, and therefore they change the days. Time is only a measurement, but the days matter." Jan forged ahead.

"The trains run on time."

"The trains *do not* run on time," Mrs. Simonson said.

"Do you want them to?"

"Of course. Who wouldn't?"

"It's rigid," Mary said.

"It's the kind of thing you *want* to be rigid. Like your heartbeat. Too much leeway and nothing works."

"This looseness you say you want is a romantic notion," Jan said.

"I don't see myself as romantic," Mary objected. "In fact, I've always hated the romantic."

"Nonsense. Review your life. See what it's created—Mariolatry. You've become a totem."

"It's the intelligence problem again. They interpreted."

"Well, what is time like for you?" Mrs. Simonson interrupted. It was hard to insert herself into the conversation; those two spoke back and forth as if they were alone. And they walked together, ahead of her.

"More like space is for you," Mary observed. "Sometimes a thing must be gotten to by waiting. But the length of the wait doesn't matter; we are not afraid of time." She paused. "Or clocks."

"And what are you here for now?" They were getting into Jan's car, a 1986 VW Rabbit. Mary had naturally gotten into the front passenger seat, leaving Mrs. Simonson to crawl into the back, which was loaded with notebooks, exercises, and extra sweaters.

"It has to do with time again. We have energy cycles in eternity, and of course there were promises. We have to change the moral order around a little." Jan shifted into gear, and they took off with a lurch. The car headed east.

"The reason I wanted to come with you," Mrs. S. said without being asked, "was because I was tired of the order in my life. Everyone has some where to go, and I—I just have endless routines, cooking and cleaning. I hate to do it anymore. You wouldn't understand that, I don't think."

"Expectations run so high at the turn of the century," Mary sighed. "As a matter of fact, I thought the women would be doing more."

"But we are. Some are. Don't go by me; I've been busy." Mrs. S. was frantically conciliatory.

"Only men strike into the wilderness," Jan said. She pulled into the passing lane.

"It's the childbirth thing," Mary said.

"Nonsense," Mrs. S. said stoutly. "There are women in the wilderness. There are pioneers. I have always been too afraid. I never even considered it, but now…. Well, the fact is, now I dream of wilderness."

"Converts?"

"Savages," Mrs. S. said wistfully. "Snakes and vines. Nakedness."

"No clocks?"

"Exactly."

"That's how it works. Sometimes you tidy things too well, so you want to move out of the tidiness. You destroy the jungle, and then you dream about the jungle." Mary did not turn around as she spoke.

"I'm not sure I would actually like it," Mrs. S. admitted.

"It's the concept that matters," Jan said drily. They were entering the Lincoln Tunnel. "What you long for is what determines what you are. Have I got that right?"

"I've never heard that, exactly," Mary said carefully. "And wouldn't it be truer that what you settle for determines you? Wouldn't that be more accurate?"

"It certainly sounds true to me," Mrs. S. said cheerfully.

When they got to Manhattan, Jan turned down the seedy streets around Tenth Avenue, until Mary said, "Stop over there." Hookers slouched against each other on both sides of the street. The Virgin pointed out a corner with three women on it.

Mary rolled down her window. "This is the Second Coming," she said pleasantly. "We are looking for someone who has been thinking of leaving the life. We need a balance. But it does not involve sex. You may think of us as a religious order. We need someone for at least a week."

"Money?" one of the hookers asked.

"This would appeal to someone with her own fantasy life. It's an adventure. And you make your own decisions."

Three pairs of eyes stared into the VW and saw a very small woman at the wheel, a woman out of a nativity play next to her, and everybody's mother in the back. No business, they calculated, unless it was kinky. Two pairs of eyes drifted back to the street, watching cars.

"Think of it as a break," the Virgin said. "Think of it as a chance to be part of a new life. A life no one else has lived."

The third prostitute—whose face was young and pretty, though her makeup was heavy-handed—tapped her foot. "My boyfriend would kill me if I just left," she said finally.

"He doesn't sound like a nice boyfriend," Mrs. S. said. "Maybe you should think about dating someone else."

The hooker grinned, a childish, flattered, happy grin. "I think you may be right," she said. "The man is a taker when I want a giver." She turned to her friends. "Tell him the last you saw me, I was getting into a car with three women, and it looked like it was gonna be a long night."

"The last I saw you," one of her friends sneered, "you were in a white dress and a wedding veil. I think I hear the bells ringing now."

"Oh, cut the crap," she said, climbing into the car. "I haven't had a vacation in a year. And I can't pull in the money like you can, so what's the point? I'm not in it for love."

"That's why you don't pull in the money." But, mollified, the friend turned away, rolling her ass in a provocative walk.

"My name is Evelyn," the hooker said. "You know, this might be what I'm looking for. Something with a little charge in it." She shook her hair (there was a lot of it) and jingled her bracelets. "Maybe religion is the ticket I've been looking for. Hey, it's a change of pace. The life can get boring, you know. No, not boring: deadening. I thought the money would help, but it's not enough money, and it's all so pathetic. I don't need glitz; I'm not your glamour girl; but there's no space for me anywhere. I'm not getting ahead, and I'm not saving myself. You're religious, you know what I mean about saving. As for me, it's the eyes. I can't stand what's in their eyes. Well, I shouldn't even look."

"I would have thought it would be their mouths," Mrs. S. said.

"Devouring, cruel, greedy."

"No. It's the eyes."

Jan drove up the West Side, staring straight ahead. "Our work starts immediately. This will be the first sign."

"Oh, yes, signs," the Virgin said, pleased. "I am, of course, partial to signs. The signs are poetry. The center remains firm, over and over. The themes remain the same; it's the details that change. They require wonders, but proof would spoil it. With proof they would despise their miracles."

Evelyn stared out alertly at the traffic. "Only the details change," she repeated. "Hey, I understand that; I was raised to read the Bible. But there's a theme there, in all these things: crucifixions, sacrifices, beheadings. Give me a clue, now: Who dies this time?"

They drove across the George Washington Bridge, circled and turned around. As they headed for the toll booths back into the city, Mrs. S. automatically started pawing through her handbag for money, but Jan drew the car off to the side and got out.

The others collected around her. Jan stared fiercely into the traffic, and they turned to stare as well. They formed a tight tableau: Jan in the back, Mrs. S. and Evelyn in front of her, and then the Virgin in front of them. In a kind of dream Mrs. S. noted how distinct everything was. Then the roads and cars shifted in her sight, and suddenly the four of them were above the toll booths, and traffic had stopped because the barriers at the tolls wouldn't rise. Mrs. S. turned her head, and at various angles she saw different lines of traffic and different roadways. She was seeing, although she didn't know it, the Brooklyn, Manhattan, and Queensboro bridges as well as the George Washington. Evelyn recognized them, and she found her own lack of surprise curious. She felt calm and happy and poised. It was as if she looked out over an edge, as if Heaven, for instance, ended in a plaza with open views.

The first earthquake struck at 4:00, followed by a much larger one at 4:01 that cracked the upper roadway of the George Washington, throwing a tractor trailer into the shallows. The Queensboro split into three sections, leaving a taxi stranded in the middle with its meter running. A train on the Manhattan Bridge slammed into an abutment that fell on the tracks. In all, nobody died on the bridges, because traffic had been so profoundly slowed by the four women floating over the entrances to all the bridges. Mysteriously, they hadn't appeared at the tunnels, and the tunnels had collapsed. Fatalities: 408.

It seemed Americans didn't travel without their videocameras. At any rate, there was footage of the four women on the bridge on all the newscasts, and the media had a field day. Was the appearance of the women a projection? What else could it be? Of course the presence of the Virgin was noticed, and the New Jersey networks reported her defection from the grotto. Was she a hoax or a symbol? The four women were not interviewed. The city itself was remarkably intact. The most dramatic destruction occurred to the World Trade Center, which lost everything above the thirty-first floor. Most tenements survived; most luxury high-rises had heavy zigzags of cracks, forcing their owners to flee. But not all of them: the very richest were spared.

While they stood elevated above each bridge, Mrs. S. and Evelyn understood the principle of simultaneity. It made empirical sense that space was porous, an idea that it seemed had occurred to them at various times before, but without such obvious evidence.

As they observed the suspended lines of angry motorists, both Mrs. S. and Evelyn felt profound well-being, a beaming contentment, a psychic adjustment at once simple and ordained. Life had never before seemed so self-evident. Mrs. S. was, behind it all, slightly reserved about such moments of revelation; she had faced revelation before and found that it faded with a vengeance. But the moments of the earthquake were the most vivid and perfect moments of their lives.

"Better even than childbirth," Mrs. S. thought. " ... than sex," Evelyn thought. Evelyn considered herself a modern, sophisticated woman. She thought she had no illusions. With the earthquake she found herself open to illusion again.

The flies had gotten out of hand. Jan's mother hung up sticky strips. She went from room to room three times a day smashing fine fat flies against the mirrors and the windows. And every day, there were more.

Cameras were constantly in evidence everywhere as the signs continued: cameras were as numerous as eyes. Jan stood to the left of the man who announced the cure for AIDS; the Virgin stood to the right of the woman who announced the discovery of a new pandemic in a fatal childbirth fever.

Mrs. S. beamed as the four of them stood on a mound in Central Park and Jan preached, "You have all lost the capacity for kindness; find it again. You learned to love yourself; now learn to love others. You have feared for yourselves; now fear for others. Don't kill. And by that I mean: Do not kill anyone. If you face killing or being killed, then die. The first rule is to harm no one, and it is not a negative rule. Where you cannot do good, do nothing, but then find a place where you can do good. Do not determine another creature's life, but provide for every creature's needs; leave their desires alone. If you live only for yourself, your life is empty, and it doesn't interest me. The greatest knowledge is not your own emotional requirements, but the requirements of other lives, of life itself, the requirements of growth and goodness. The unnecessary pain you inflict on any creature will be your own inheritance. The hell I choose to give you is your own mind for eternity, silent and alone. Love yourselves, yes, but love every child, every creature who cries out or moans or looks with longing. The degree of your love is the degree of your salvation."

The crowd looked at her speculatively; they had seen her on the news. But their eyes turned automatically to Mary, who was more recognizable. Some came to worship her, having followed her from the grotto in New Jersey, but some came hoping to see how the trick was done.

"They've been given everything; they are free from hunger. So they eat potato chips and watch TV." Jan was bitter, even angry, as she walked through a street fair. Smells of food after food pushed toward them: rich, fat-laden. Jan strode through, pushing people out of the way. "Only the hungry should eat!" she cried. As if on cue, a few homeless people snaked their way through the crowd, creeping around her.

There were cameras at the fair, bright lights and microphones. "What about feeding the hungry?" a reporter asked a vendor.

"I feed the hungry," the vendor said, squinting into the lights. He held up a slice of pizza. "Papa's Pizza," he said, handing slices to the hands outstretched before him. "Every pie you buy, we give a slice to the homeless." He grinned, and he almost laughed. "We don't even charge more; we give our profits to the poor." Hands reached out to him, and he turned to the camera. "Papa's Pizza. Mulberry Street. Be nice to your belly, and be nice to your conscience."

They slept in Evelyn's apartment in the West Forties. It amazed Mrs. S. that Jan and the Virgin did sleep, although only five hours each.

Mrs. S. and Evelyn were exhausted; they had been together three days, but it felt like much longer. They were always moving about, swept up in a ceaseless campaign.

"When they talk about *good*, they sound so certain," Mrs. S. complained, "as if there were an obvious good. I've had children; I know all good is relative."

"But you get the idea."

"The idea of goodness," Mrs. S. sighed. "On one level, of course I do. But it's a stretch, isn't it? To do good for one's entire lifetime." She paused, and they both considered this, their chins lowered.

Evelyn was thinking out loud. "It was something, wasn't it? Watching her march through all that food, and they all started handing it out."

"Loaves and fishes."

"I'm perfectly aware," Evelyn snapped.

Mrs. S., who by now was used to Evelyn's snapping, continued to muse on her own. "Jan was angry."

"Pissed as hell."

"If God has emotions, then God has psychology," Mrs. S. said softly.

Evelyn stared. "Unless it's just another sign."

Mrs. S. nodded. "Interesting."

The flies were present everywhere, not just in Ellen's house. The press reported on it as due to an unusual warm spell in late October; a new generation of larvae had formed.

"She doesn't even call," Ellen said softly.

Michael sipped his coffee and snapped his newspaper. "You know what she says. She says she's God."

Ellen sighed and looked out the window, which was speckled with the moving bodies of flies. "I would have gone with her, Michael," she said with real grief. "I would go to her now."

Michael shook his paper again; his eyes stayed put. "Just think about it, Ellen. How could she be God?" Ellen noted how his voice was aggrieved.

"Where do gods come," Ellen asked, "but from the people?"

Michael turned the page. His mouth twitched.

Jan and the Virgin were still consulting in the spare room, where they had been shut up for hours. Left to themselves, Mrs. S. and Evelyn had a crisis of faith.

"The thing is," Evelyn said, "I want to believe it, but I'm not sure why. I mean, I would very much like to be a fanatic about something. Jan and Mary—well, they reached out to me, they chose me; I feel almost obligated. I'm just not sure whether I want to be on the inside of this. Have you heard how Jan keeps saying that we must be ready for the sacrifice?"

"I'm sure it's just a metaphor."

"How often does she talk in metaphors?"

Mrs. S. frowned. "But I believe in her," she said.

Evelyn shrugged and then drew a lipstick from her purse. "I think there's a price for believing things. This one will be high."

"You're not going to back out now?"

"Oh, no," Evelyn sighed, snapping her lipstick shut and checking her lips, "it's too late now for that. I've never been a tease, not me. In for a dime, in for a dollar."

"I worry about my husband and daughter," Mrs. S. admitted. "But not as much as I should. Still, there are people I have loved, and it frightens me: Who will be saved?"

"I intend to be saved."

"I would like them all to be saved. It seems sad, now, when you look at them and wonder how they will end."

"You see? That's what I mean. Fanatics don't worry about such things. Theories get turned to emotions with fanatics, and that's what I want. I want to be so crazy about the thought of something that nothing matters, not even death matters. Well, you can see these people are not usual. They have a plan, and they have a purpose, and they're looking ahead to something they can already see. That's better than anyone I know, and the earth seems to bow down before them. You can feel the air's charged, can't you?"

"Yes, the air is charged. The back of my neck tingles. I can feel the hairs stand on end."

"I feel it," Evelyn lowered her voice, "like sex."

The door opened, and Jan and the Virgin came out. They had so much light around them that Evelyn had to squint, and Mrs. S. felt again the sense of being on some sort of edge, as she had at the bridge.

"The Rapture has begun," the Virgin said kindly. "We are calling the saved." Mrs. S. turned to see the world begin to extend itself out from the window. She grabbed Evelyn's hand, and together they felt a terror that had at its core a beautiful, thrilling enticement. It was only at the edges—and evaporating rapidly—that Mrs. S. heard her own sad question, "Who will be saved?" The sad sound of it was growing dim. Evelyn felt exalted, and her eyes rolled back in her head briefly before she dropped Mrs. S.'s hand and moved with her arms outstretched to Jan. A wind seemed to pour out from Jan's mouth and envelop them all.

At the same moment, all the flies died. Ellen was sitting at the kitchen table, reading the clips about Jan that she'd torn out of the papers.

She could remember nothing out of the ordinary about the pregnancy or the birth. She had gone over it a hundred times, trying to find something in herself or in Michael that would explain it all. "Mothers

amcontent.com/pod-product-compliance
Source LLC
urg PA
700030726
300002B/582

of criminals," she thought, "must feel like this—so unexpectedly adrift without the idea of their child."

She began to sweep the flies up when a wind from an open window blew them into a whirlwind. She looked out and saw a man raise his hand up against the radiance. Something in the quality of the light convinced her that Jan was coming.

She straightened her back, dusted her skirts, and opened the door. The wind was full of voices.

www.in
Lightnin
Chamber
CBHW02
47498C

of criminals," she thought, "must feel like this—so unexpectedly adrift without the idea of their child."

She began to sweep the flies up when a wind from an open window blew them into a whirlwind. She looked out and saw a man raise his hand up against the radiance. Something in the quality of the light convinced her that Jan was coming.

She straightened her back, dusted her skirts, and opened the door. The wind was full of voices.

www.ingramcontent.com/pod-product-compliance
Lightning Source LLC
Chambersburg PA
CBHW020700030726
47498CB00002B/582